I0456905

gabriel

FROM GRACE

KRIS NORRIS

OTHER BOOKS BY KRIS NORRIS

SINGLES

CENTERFOLD

KEEPING FAITH

IRON WILL

MY SOUL TO KEEP

RICOCHET

ROPE'S END

SERIES

'TIL DEATH

1 - DEADLY VISION

2 - DEADLY OBSESSION

3 - DEADLY DECEPTION

BROTHERHOOD PROTECTORS ~ Elle James

1 - MIDNIGHT RANGER

2 – CARVED IN ICE

3 - GOING IN BLIND

COLLATERAL DAMAGE

1 - FORCE OF NATURE

DARK PROPHECY

GABRIEL

FROM GRACE

KRIS NORRIS

Gabriel

Copyright © 2018, Kris Norris

Edited by Chris Allen-Riley and Jessica Bimberg

Cover Art by Kris Norris

Published by Kris Norris

Updated September, 2018

This is a work of fiction. All characters, places and events are from the author's imagination and should not be confused with fact. Any resemblance to persons, living or dead, events or places is purely coincidental.

All rights reserved. No part of this publication may be reproduced in any material form, whether by printing, photocopying, scanning or otherwise without the written permission of the author, Kris Norris.

To everyone who's had the courage to take a leap of faith. Set the bar high, or you'll never reach the stars.

CHAPTER ONE

"An angel?" Kei scrubbed a hand down his face as he tilted his head forward. "I summoned a fucking angel?"

Fire licked across his skin, the tiny arcs flashing bright in the darkness. Anger fueled the flames, burning the yellow wisps into a deep crimson. Of all the bloody screw ups...

Kei crossed the cemetery, stopping just shy of the symbol he'd inscribed on the ground. Black ash coated the parched dirt, traces of blood baked into the grooves scored on the land. He stared at the man crouched within the circle, muscles straining, creamy skin gleaming in the moonlight. Creamy-white feathers fluttered in the breeze, his wings still unfurled across his back. Sweat beaded the guy's flesh, trailing down the strong curve of his spine. Summonings weren't pleasurable for demons. For angels —they killed more often than they succeeded.

Kei frowned. He'd cast a fire enchantment. Used more than a bit of his blood and all the damn power he could spare as payment. A desperate last effort to prolong his life, just long enough to hunt and kill the fallen bastard who'd cursed him to this fucking realm. The god damn human world. The one entity who could destroy this dimension and a dozen more like it if Kei didn't end the war before it began. He'd expected a blood demon. A soulless vessel he could possess until he'd found his prey. Preserve what little strength he had left before the final battle.

And he'd fucking deserved the creature. Fire enchantments were tricky. Risky. He would have gladly accepted death as a suitable recourse for a botched attempt. But he'd gotten every intonation and ancient pronunciation right. Had known the moment he'd finished, he'd been successful.

And yet, he'd somehow summoned an angel.

Kei crossed his arms over his chest as he braced his feet a shoulder width apart. "Don't suppose you're really a blood demon in disguise?"

The man's ragged breathing filled the air, his head finally lifting enough to meet Kei's gaze. Lines creased his forehead, his clear blue eyes wide.

Kei shook his head, leaning his hip against a tombstone. "Guess that's a no." He held up his hand, hoping to stop the guy when he looked as if he was going to try to stand. "I wouldn't do that just yet unless you like falling. Wouldn't want to bruise that pretty-boy face of yours."

The angelic man glared at him, pushing to his feet before stumbling across the circle. He hit one of the stone crosses, the dull thud echoing through the graveyard. He sagged against the headstone, red slashing across his cheeks.

Kei tsked. "Can't say I didn't warn you."

"Silence, demon, before I strike you down for simply standing there."

Kei chuckled. "Yeah, you might find that whole smiting thing a bit difficult. Summonings tend to drain your life force. And I didn't use near enough energy to fuel an angel." He cocked his head to the side. "You got a name?"

The man clenched his jaw, drawing himself up despite the ways his limbs shook from the strain. "I'm an angel, not stupid. Names are powerful."

"Right. Because that's really what I'd been hoping for. A self-righteous asshole with enough soul to fill this godforsaken cemetery. That was my plan all along." He sighed. "The name's Kei."

"I don't care."

"Jackass it is."

The man sneered. "I won't fall for your tricks."

"No, you chose to fall from the fucking sky instead." Kei closed the distance, wondering when the guy would notice he was buck-ass nude. "How the hell did you get here, anyway? And what did you do with my demon?"

"What did I..." The man arched a brow, his wings fluttering against the stone as the wind picked up, tossing dried leaves into the air like confetti. "And here I thought you might be slightly more intelligent than most demons. You just said you summoned me. There's a blood token carved into the ground. You figure it out."

"I cast a fire enchantment. For a blood demon." Kei smirked. "I'll admit, ancient spells aren't my specialty, but even I'm not incompetent enough to fuck it up to the point I get an angel as compensation. Why are you really here? Who sent you?"

"Again. *You* summoned *me*."

"Are you deaf? I said I summoned a blood demon. Fuck!" Kei turned, taking a few angry steps away before spinning. "Why would I raise the one being who can't help me?"

"Since when do demons require help?"

Kei blew out an exasperated breath, twisting his palm face up before allowing his magic to spark to life. A flicking light appeared above his hand, the heat warning his skin. "Fire mage, jackass."

"You said you were a demon."

"I said I summoned one. You decided I was a demon." Kei allowed the flame to bounce in his hand before racing up his arm then down the other, finally winking out. The feel of his power soothed some of the rawness coursing through him, though the resulting wave of dizziness was just another reminder of how much energy he'd sacrificed. How weak he really was. "Don't suppose you'll surrender your soul long enough for me to possess your body—use you as a vessel to hunt down a nasty bastard that needs exterminating?"

The man shook his head, finally glancing down. Kei smiled. Despite the fact the guy was far too pure for his tastes, Kei had to admit he was more than attractive. Messy brown hair tousled about his head, strong smooth features that curved in perfect symmetry—the man was beautiful. Breathtaking, in fact. Even his body seemed flawless—pale skin covering lean muscles that flexed with every small movement. If it weren't for the fact the angel had been drained of his grace, Kei bet his ass the other man would be a tough opponent to best. That's if the guy would actually fight. Hell, who was he kidding? Without direction from a much higher power, the guy wouldn't lift a finger to help Kei, worthy mission or not.

Kei slumped his shoulders as he braced his weight on one of the gravestones. "Of all the creatures I could have gotten by mistake, it had to be you."

"Do you really expect me to believe this was an accident?"

"I don't really give a fuck what you believe, jackass. I wanted a blood demon."

"Stop calling me that."

"Then give me something else to call you." Kei snorted. "Bloody hell, it's not like I can kill you. Even weakened, you've got far too much raw power for me to challenge. Especially when I haven't come close to recovering from my offering." He raked a hand through his hair. "And why the hell would I summon an angel? I need a creature that can kill, not a holier-than-thou prick who can't so much as nick someone's skin without having a moral crisis."

The man straightened, his chest thickening as he drew himself up. Kei did his best to ignore the way the man's cock rose, heavy and hard, between his legs. The end shiny in the waning light. Damn it. Now wasn't the time to get distracted, especially by the one being he couldn't have.

"You're mistaken if you think I'm incapable of destroying you the moment I regain my power." The man smiled at Kei. "Even my soul can stand the pain of seeing the rest of your blood stain the ground."

"Great. I cast a spell for a demon and get the one angel

who doesn't seem to have an issue with slaying a mage. Must be my lucky day."

"Then perhaps you shouldn't have cast the spell at all."

"I didn't summon..." Kei cursed under his breath. He'd failed. One last chance to stop a war before it destroyed a thousand worlds, and he'd somehow failed without ever getting close enough to try. He met the man's heated gaze. "If I had enough strength to send you back..." He huffed. "Guess you're stuck here until I recharge, though I'm not sure exactly how to return you, seeing as I didn't ask for your presence in the first place."

"Like you'd send me back."

"With pleasure."

The man's grim expression faltered. "Why did you summon a blood demon? You're a mage. Far more powerful than some empty shell of a beast."

"I needed something I could control—a creature that could blend in, not to mention take one hell of a beating. A way to conserve my power without abandoning my quest."

"Quest?" A harsh laugh rumbled free. "Since when is killing a quest?"

"Since it's the only way to prevent a war that won't end until every living creature in every damn realm has been purged from existence."

"War?" The man tilted his head, staring at Kei as if seeing him for the first time. "Who is it you seek?"

"Bastard's got a lot of names. You'd know him as Abaddon." Kei arched one brow. "I believe he used to be one of yours before he fell. Only, he chose his destiny."

"Abaddon? That can't be. He died when he was cast..."

Disbelief shaped his features before he motioned to Kei. "Where's your army, Mage?"

"Why do you think I tried to summon a demon?"

"You're alone?" The man's mouth pinched tight, his focus shifting to the symbols still visible within the circle. "Are you mad?"

"From the moment you appeared."

The man sighed, his gaze finding Kei's again. "Gabriel."

Kei frowned. "What's that?"

"My name. It's Gabriel. And you just got far more than you bargained for."

Kei's mouth hinged open as he stared at the angel—Gabriel. Surely, the man was lying. He couldn't truly be who he claimed.

Kei drew himself up. "Gabriel? As in the archangel? All-fucking-powerful? Can kill damn near anything with a snap of his fingers...Gabriel?" He shook his head. "This isn't funny. Getting an angel is one thing. And despite the fact I sacrificed more energy than was wise, there's no way it was enough to summon a being that strong."

"Do you think I'd give you my name lightly?"

Kei backed up, his gaze sweeping the length of Gabe's body. Muscles flexed and released under his perusal, the pure beauty of his form sending a shiver down Kei's spine. He glanced away, rerunning every step he'd taken. Every word he'd uttered before he'd finished the spell, and somehow gotten...him.

Kei shook his head. "It simply can't be."

Gabe lifted his chin, a knowing smile tilting his lips. "Why would I lie about who I am, Mage?"

"The name's Kei. And I can think of a dozen different

reasons as to why you'd lie to me, least of all because you're pissed." He pushed his hand through his hair, wondering what in the hell he'd done to deserve this.

Gabe's smile faded, the muscle in his temple jumping as he clenched his jaw.

Kei raised his hand in seeming defeat. "Fine. You're… Gabriel. Archangel and current pain in my ass." He crossed his arms over his chest. "So, why are you really here?"

"Are we really going to argue this, again? You summoned me."

"And again, I shouldn't have gotten an angel, let alone you. The spell was fairly specific. And the last time I checked, demon and angel were pretty much opposites."

Gabe copied Kei's stance, crossing his massive arms over his chest, apparently obvious to how the simple act made his cock jut out from between his legs. He looked at the sigil carved into the ground. His brow furrowed, a hushed curse mumbling free.

Kei chuckled. "Easy, Gabe. Wouldn't want you to start sinning so soon."

Gabe glared at him, making his way over to one of the symbols on the ground. "If this is your idea of specific, you have much to learn, Ma…" He sighed. "Kei. Do you have any idea what kind of power is hidden within some of these markings?"

"Just followed the instructions, buddy. And for the record, I didn't really think I'd survive the procedure, so I didn't spend too much time worrying about what every damn symbol meant. It was supposed to grant me a worthy vessel. That's all that mattered."

Gabe shook his head. "I suggest you take better care in

the future because this set of tokens has more than one translation. As for a worthy vessel..." He looked at Kei over his shoulder, tsking. "You're lucky you didn't summon Lucifer, himself, with the mix of angelic and demonic sigils you carved into the earth."

"Right, because like I said...today is definitely my lucky day."

"I'd think *not* summoning my older brother is considered extremely lucky."

Kei groaned as he walked over to Gabriel, making a point of studying the markings before shrugging. "Whatever you say. But the fact still remains... I never should have been able to summon you in the first place. Your power alone puts you in a completely different league. It doesn't make any sense." He blew out an exasperated breath. "Christ, I don't know how you even survived. But regardless, looks like you're stuck here for a while. Assuming you know the ritual to unsummon you, because that..." He waved at the circle. "Is all I could dig up on this particular spell. And it was harder than hell to decipher. I never planned on sending that demon back."

"It would appear you didn't plan on much of anything...other than dying during your ceremony."

Kei drew a shaky breath, doing his best to calm the fire licking just below the surface of his skin. If he'd known angels were this irritating, he'd have walked away and left Gabe to figure everything out for himself.

Kei motioned to the man. "You sure your brothers didn't give you the boot? Because I'd understand why they'd want to kick you out of their little club. You're annoying as hell."

Gabe straightened, his sheer presence making the air

feel charged. "Only my Father or another archangel would have the strength to cast me out. I doubt it's something I'd forget."

Kei backed up a few steps. "Easy, buddy. I wasn't serious. Damn, you angels don't have much of a sense of humor, do you?" He arched a brow. "So, this is what an archangel looks like."

"What were you expecting?"

"Clothes, for one thing. Maybe more refined, less warrior worthy."

Gabe's frown intensified. "Michael isn't the only one among us who fights."

Kei chuckled. "Got some brother issues, Gabe? All I said was that you're not what I expected. Though, honestly, never thought much about angels. The one I've met isn't exactly a benchmark of greatness."

Gabe's brow furrowed as a flash of white fire gleamed in his eyes. "If what you claim is true, Abaddon isn't an angel." He turned away, adding, "At least, not anymore."

Kei felt the mixture of pain and anguish churning inside Gabriel as if the emotions were his. He rolled his shoulders against the unusual sensation, hoping it was simply a byproduct of sacrificing so much of his power. His blood. He closed the distance, nudging the other man. "I'll make you a deal."

Gabe snorted. "I don't make deals. Demons do."

Kei cursed under his breath. The jackass was infuriating at best. "It's a figure of speech. What I was going to say was...you don't second guess everything I claim, and I'll believe you in return."

Gabe drew his brows together. "I'm an angel. Why wouldn't you believe what I say?"

"Fuck. What you *are* is a piece of work. And incredibly naive. Fine. We'll discuss this later, but for now...we'd best find you some clothes and get the hell out of here before that heavenly glow of yours attracts every damn paranormal being within fifty miles. And I'm still not strong enough to start picking fights with werewolves and demons who have a hankering for angel blood."

"I don't need you to defend me, Mage."

"It's either me, or..." Kei chuckled. "Right. There isn't anyone else. Just...stick close. Full moon's not that far away, and with Samhain this close, evil is a bit stronger than usual."

Gabe huffed but fell in behind Kei as he stalked across the cemetery, the echoed cry of a wolf ringing through the surrounding trees. He could figure out their next move later—after he'd recharged. Had half a chance of surviving a confrontation. Until then, he'd babysit Gabriel. Even if the man didn't think he needed it.

CHAPTER TWO

"Oh for fuck's sake, Gabriel. Don't stand near the damn lamplight. We're in the middle of town. Do you want everyone to see you?"

Gabriel glared at the man off to his right. Kei. A fire mage, or so he claimed. Though it was clear now the man wasn't a demon, there were other entities that could mimic Kei's fire abilities, all of which were far more dangerous. Far darker. And until Gabriel regained more of his grace, he wouldn't be able to tell for sure.

He sighed. Though his interactions on Earth had been...limited, he'd encountered enough sorcerers to know they often walked a fine line when it came to moral fortitude, usually straying into the shadows rather than staying in the light. And Gabriel wasn't getting his hopes up that Kei was any different.

Gabriel crossed his arms over his chest. "Unlike you, Mage, I don't make a habit of skulking in the dark."

"Unless you want me to go back to calling you jackass, it's Kei." Kei cocked an eyebrow at him, his gaze traveling the length of Gabriel's body. "And if you want to walk down the street like a human, then mask your damn wings and put on the shirt I gave you. Unless you like strolling around with nothing but some pants covering you." He snorted. "I thought you angels were all about secrecy? Hiding what you were and some bullshit? Not messing with humans." He waved at him. "Anyone with half a brain can tell those wings are real. Fuck, they're practically glowing. Actually, *you're* practically glowing."

Gabriel clenched his jaw. While he knew the other man wasn't a match for his sheer power, Gabriel didn't want to confess it required every bit of strength he had just to walk. If he admitted how weak he felt, it'd give Kei a chance to overtake him. Use some ancient spell to steal what was left of Gabriel's grace.

He firmed his stance. "I wasn't the one who orchestrated all of this."

"And I was? As I've told you more than a dozen times, I summoned a blood demon. Blame this unfortunate pairing on a higher power than me, buddy, because I did everything right. Something else intervened, whether you want to acknowledge that fact or not." He snorted. "Poetic justice, I suppose. Obviously, my life wasn't fucked up enough, already."

"So you claim, and I doubt the shirt will fit."

"Leave the damn front open if you have to. That's better than what you've got. Which is nothing. Now, hide your damn wings and get out of the light until I can get us somewhere safe for the night. There're more than a few creatures tracking us. Well, you, anyway."

Gabriel muttered under his breath, moving away from the soft glow of the streetlight as he headed for the shadows that lined the sidewalk. Darkness gathered around him, and he resisted the urge to brighten it with a hint of his power. Chase away the evil that lurked in the hidden recesses of this world—even if he was the only one who felt it.

He glanced at Kei. The man hadn't stopped scouring the street and surrounding buildings since they'd left the cemetery. As if he were searching for something—other than the obvious perils he'd already mentioned. Someone specific. Though it didn't look as if the mage was hoping to find whoever it was. In fact, the sorcerer seemed... restless.

Gabriel turned away. He didn't need to fuel the connection between them any more than it already was. Strengthen the link created by Kei's spell. It was a byproduct of the summoning—a fusion of Kei's life force with his own. And the only reason Gabriel had survived the ordeal. He'd had more than a few brothers and sisters die in ancient rituals like the one Kei had performed, and Gabriel knew he'd been lucky, though it had obviously cost the mage. No wonder the other man appeared weak. Gabriel could only imagine how much of his power Kei had given in the hopes of gaining his prize. It also meant Gabriel was more than tied to the man. He was bound. Physically. Emotionally. Even now, he felt the heat of Kei's magic scratch at his skin. As if the fire was beneath his flesh and not the sorcerer's. And their connection would only grow stronger as their energy increased. As daunting as Gabriel's power was, even he wouldn't be able to break the enchantment. They'd be stuck with each other until they'd finished this 'quest', or until Kei sent him back.

Gabriel glanced at the other man. As much as he tried

to tell himself the guy was lying, Gabriel didn't sense it. In fact, despite what his head screamed at him, he felt Kei's honesty. His despair at his apparent failure. Hell, Gabriel felt the man's soul, and it wasn't one tainted with darkness. It felt—pure. As pure as any human's could be. And Kei was essentially that. Human, but with…gifts.

Gabriel's cock stirred within the confines of the denim Kei had given him. Just Gabriel's luck. The sorcerer would have called to him before the spell. Long brown hair that hung in an unruly mess about his head. Strong, rippling muscles that seemed to flex with every small movement. The man looked more like a warrior than a sorcerer, his shoulders nearly as wide as Gabriel's. But it was Kei's eyes that intrigued Gabriel the most. Deep green, they rivaled the color of the leaves that rustled in the wind beside the sacred pool. The kind of gaze that drew Gabriel in and refused to let go.

He shook away the thoughts. Obviously having Kei's power pulse inside him… It was more than distracting. It was dangerous. And a road Gabriel couldn't travel. Especially if the man lived up to Gabriel's assumptions.

Abaddon.

Gabriel prayed Kei was wrong. That once Gabriel had regained his power, Kei would reveal the truth. One that didn't involve a man Gabriel had once called brother. A man he'd thought had perished centuries ago when he'd chosen to fall to Earth. Chosen to walk amidst the shadows. Though if Kei was telling the truth…

Kei grabbed his wrist and yanked him farther into the grayed shadows, snapping Gabriel back from his thoughts. The mage chuckled. "You are one stubborn bastard, aren't you?" He shook his head. "Your wings, Gabriel."

Gabriel took a deep breath, mentally assessing if he could spare the energy to make the glamour work, when Kei tugged him against his chest, before he spun, shoving Gabriel's back against the wall as he palmed the surface on either side of Gabriel's body. Kei pressed in close, sparring a quick glance over his shoulder before turning back.

The mage leaned in, his breath caressing Gabriel's jaw. "Put your hands on my waist and look as if you want to pull me even closer."

"What the...get off me—"

Kei silenced him with a brush of his mouth over his. "There's a water demon at the end of the street, and I sure as shit don't have the power to go up against it right now. And with you practically casting a fucking spotlight on the fact you're an angel..." He looked over his shoulder again. "It'd be best for both of us if it just continued on its way. Didn't give us a second glance. And there's nothing like public shows of affection to make people uncomfortable. Even folks possessed by demons."

Gabriel stiffened. He didn't have the strength to wage a battle. Not yet. Hell, he couldn't even put up a glamour. "How do you know it's a demon?"

"Let's just say that my last encounter with Abaddon—the one that banished me here—had a few lasting side effects. Though I doubt he planned it that way. One of which enables me to see the demon beneath the flesh. It's not pretty, but...comes in handy."

"That's impossible unless he..." Gabriel sucked in a harsh breath. It couldn't be. Even Abaddon wouldn't curse someone with a ritual as evil as what Kei seemed to be alluding to.

Gabriel stared the mage in the eyes. "Are you saying he used a demon blood spell on you? Tried to rip out your soul and feed upon it?"

"You seem surprised. Perhaps you don't know the man as well as you think. Thankfully, it didn't quite work." Kei eased back ever so slightly. "I can still see your wings, Gabe. You got a death wish I'm unaware of?"

Gabriel clenched his jaw.

Kei stared at him, then huffed. "Shit, you can't, can you? You're not strong enough."

Gabriel sneered at him. "Don't think that I'm admitting I'm weak. I could still kill you."

Kei rolled his eyes. "Right, you can kill me, but you can't retract your damn wings."

"Despite how it might appear, casting a convincing glamour to mask my purity is extremely taxing. A feat requiring a great deal of power. Normally, I can toss one up without thinking about it—"

"But you're out of juice. Fuck." Kei sparred a quick peek down the street. "Damn it, it's still coming this way. And there's nowhere else to go." He met Gabriel's stare. "Two choices. I challenge it, or I give you the energy you need to hide those damn feathers. Pray it walks past. Either way, I won't be much help for a while. I haven't recharged nearly enough."

Gabriel furrowed his brow. "You expect me to believe you'd risk your life for me?"

"Not every being other than your self-righteous brothers and sisters are evil, buddy. And I didn't exactly ask for this." He glanced away for a moment. "I hate to admit it, but...not sure I'd even buy you enough time to get away if I challenge it. I'm..." His voice faded. "Oh, fuck it."

Kei moved one hand to the back of Gabriel's head, spearing his fingers through Gabriel's hair as he fisted the strands, holding Gabriel's head still. He closed the distance, giving Gabriel a gentle brush of his mouth before sealing his lips to Gabriel's. Gabriel gasped, moaning when the man slid his tongue inside, tangling it with his. Spicy heat engulfed his senses, followed by a rush of pure power.

Kei hummed, deepening the kiss as more of his life force curled through Gabriel, coiling heat low in his core. Pleasure peaked his cock against his pants, the hard press of Kei's shaft drawing a muffled moan from deep inside. Kei moved his other hand to Gabriel's back, slowly tracing up his spine until he grazed the edge of his wings.

Gabriel's breath caught. He wasn't sure if Kei knew an angel's wings were incredibly sensitive, or if the man just liked touching, but be damned if it didn't make the world spin. Gabriel pressed slightly against Kei, tightening his hold around the man's waist. The sorcerer's muscles tensed, flexing beneath Gabriel's hands before he slowly eased back, his forehead resting against Gabriel's. Gabriel blinked open his eyes as tiny sparks flashed across Kei's skin, bursting into shards of warm, orange light before winking out. The mage's breath mixed with his, the rough exhalations matching Gabriel's.

Energy surged along his flesh, swirling inward as he used the power to mask his appearance, grunting as his wings trembled, fluttering wildly against the gray stone behind him before retracting, leaving a light sheen of sweat along his skin. He drew in a few shaky breaths, relaxing slightly as the straining in his muscles eased. He glanced at his arms, watching as the last of his golden glow sank beneath the surface.

Kei clenched his jaw, moving his hand to the wall again, bracing it beside Gabriel's head as footsteps echoed close by. Kei held firm, shifting his eyes slightly as a man moved into view beyond Kei's shoulder. The guy glanced at them, frowning as he mumbled something under his breath, turning away in seeming disgust. A shudder raced along Kei's limbs as his head bowed forward against Gabriel's shoulder.

He palmed Kei's chest, holding back a hum of approval as the man's muscles jumped beneath his touch. The firm strum of the sorcerer's heartbeat thrummed against his fingertips, the rather erratic rhythm matching Gabriel's. He pushed against the man's torso, cursing the sudden jolt of lust that didn't want Kei to disengage. That mocked Gabriel's resolve to remain distant. "You can move, now."

Kei lifted his head, pain creasing the edges of his mouth. "Wait until it's out of sight, and we're sure it's not tricking us."

Gabriel pursed his lips, looking up the street, waiting until the stranger had crossed the road and disappeared down another alley. He let his head fall against the building, hoping the simple act would loosen in the tight feeling in his chest. He glanced at Kei, raising his brow in question. "That good enough for you?"

"Must you be such an ass?" Kei twisted, obviously checking for himself, before he nodded. "We should try to avoid any further contact until we're able to hold our own."

"There's no *us* once I regain my strength." The lie

tasted bitter on Gabriel's tongue, but he'd be damned if he'd admit he was bound. That leaving wasn't an option. The less Kei knew for now, the better. At least, until Gabriel could face any threat unaided.

Kei flashed him a cocky grin. "I never said there was. I was merely making a suggestion, seeing as neither of us is at full strength. Though if you think you can take on a horde of demons or werewolves alone...." He grunted, shoulders slumping as he dragged in a ragged breath. "How long can you hold that glamour?"

"A while." Gabriel sighed. He wouldn't be feeling half as strong if the other man hadn't given up more of his energy. He stared the sorcerer, noting the tremble in Kei's hands as he fisted them against the brick. Dark smudges now lined his eyes, and the heat he'd sensed beneath Kei's skin had dimmed.

Gabriel considered probing their connection—allowing the mage's thoughts to invade his, but decided against it. He couldn't risk deepening their link until he'd unearthed the truth. Until the ghosted feel of the man's lips had faded. "You okay?"

Kei shoved off the wall, taking half a dozen shaky steps back. "Fine. But we've still got a few more blocks to go before we reach my place. We should head out." He turned, tripping onto one knee—his hand smacking the pavement as it bridged the rest of his weight.

Gabriel darted over to him, kneeling at his side. He brushed back the man's messy locks, frowning at Kei's obvious pain. "You gave me too much."

Kei snorted. "You needed to mask your appearance. What good is holding some back if we're both dead?"

"What if that demon had recognized me for what I am?"

"Then it would have killed me, and it still wouldn't matter."

Gabriel blew out a long breath. "Why did you help me? You could have run. Saved yourself."

Kei glanced at him, the smugness Gabriel had expected to see in Kei's expression noticeably absent. "I'm far from innocent, but even I don't want the blood of an angel on my conscience, let alone an archangel. Especially since you're here because of me...even if it was accidental." He drew in a few ragged pants. "You should go ahead. Second street on the left. Halfway down there's a red door. It's magically sealed but with your improved energy supply, I'm sure you can find a way around the ward. I'll follow when I can."

Gabriel cocked his brow. The man certainly didn't make staying removed easy. He shook his head. "I still think you're hiding the truth from me, Kei, but..." He wrapped his arm under Kei's, levering him up. "I'll help you get to this refuge you seek. Payback for what you did."

Kei grunted, the strain to simply move his feet forward painfully obvious. "And here I thought you were still pissed because I'd summoned you."

"You didn't have to give me your power. It was actually quite foolish, considering I could kill you with nothing more than my hands right now."

"You. Abaddon. My future seems to hold the same end, regardless."

Gabriel studied Kei. If the man was lying about Abaddon's involvement, Gabriel certainly couldn't sense it. Though that didn't mean Kei was honorable. Or even trying to do as he'd claimed.

Gabriel balanced their weight as they moved slowly along the sidewalk. "Thank you."

Kei chuckled. "Don't thank me, yet. Hell, we haven't even gotten clear of the street."

Gabriel sighed, ignoring the way the man's body felt dangerously right against his. This was nothing more than erasing a debt. Helping Kei in return for his kindness. It didn't mean anything. And it sure as hell didn't mean Gabriel cared.

CHAPTER THREE

"Is this the door you mentioned?"

Kei dragged his gaze up from the sidewalk, doing his best to focus on the area in front of him as Gabriel's voice wavered in and out of pitch. Shapes swam across his vision, nothing but a red blur truly registering. Fuck, he felt weak. If it weren't for the other man shouldering most of his weight, he'd have passed out beneath the lamplight. Even with the angel's help, he'd barely managed to put one foot in front of the other—drag his ass home.

He leaned more heavily against Gabe, wishing he had another option. It seemed every moment he spent next to the guy affected him on some deeper level. As if he could sense the man's thoughts. Desires. And damn if he didn't agree with at least some of them.

He grinned. Seemed Gabe wasn't quite as pure as Kei had first thought, the man's mind replaying their kiss more than a few times. Not that Kei had been able to think about anything else, either. And he knew, if given the chance, he'd kiss the man again. Hell, he wanted to do far more than merely kiss Gabriel.

Gabe cleared his throat, giving Kei a shake. "Did you hear me? Are we here? I can sense strands of magic, but..." He sighed. "I'm still not strong enough to be certain it's yours, though there's something familiar about the way it pulses."

Kei squinted, finally getting the scenery to stabilize long enough to recognize his door. "Home sweet home." He swallowed as his voice cracked on the last word before nodding at the small gate. "I can unseal the door from there."

Gabe didn't speak, just moved forward, seemingly oblivious to how slowly they covered the short expanse of pavement. Kei touched the metal frame, uttering a few words as his barrier snapped and hissed, flaring sparks of crimson flame into the air before winking out. A small surge of power sank beneath his flesh, making him acutely aware of how much strength it took to stand, and he leaned into Gabe, waiting to see if he'd simply fall on his face.

Gabe shuffled Kei's weight, the man's chest bracing most of it as he somehow eased them forward. "I sincerely hope you don't make a habit of giving up nearly all of your power. Surprised you're actually still alive."

Kei snorted. "Don't usually have to save an angel."

"You didn't have to..." Gabe chuckled. "Let's just get you inside so you can rest. You're not exactly light."

"This coming from a man who's even bigger than I am."

"Who's also managing to walk on his own."

"Pretty damn sure that's my energy flowing inside you, buddy."

"Must you always have the last word?" Gabe tightened his hold. "Almost there."

The door creaked as it swung open then closed, the sound muffled as Kei scuffed his feet on the wood floors, somehow staying upright until Gabe pivoted, gently placing him on a couch. He groaned when his back hit the cushions, fatigue drawing him under as he closed his eyes. A hand brushed his hair from his face, and he forced his eyelids open—catching his breath as he stared into Gabe's blue gaze. Fuck, the man's eyes were mesmerizing. Dare he say…heavenly?

Gabe's mouth quirked into a smile. "You're not at all what I expected."

"You did think I was a demon."

"Besides that. You're…" His voice faded, a delightful crease forming above the bridge of his nose. "Rest. I'll fortify the dwelling—ensure we'll be safe until you can stand without falling."

Kei shook his head, trying to push onto his elbows only to collapse again. "I'll cast a spell—"

"You can't even sit up."

"You need to conserve your power. Might take you a while to recharge down here."

"I'm an archangel. I think I can inscribe a few symbols on the windows and doors without draining myself." Gabe pressed both hands on Kei's shoulders, keeping him pinned to the couch. "I put my faith in you when I followed you home. Now, give me yours."

Kei forced himself to swallow, wondering when the hell his throat had gotten so dry. He glanced at where

Gabriel's hands cupped his shoulders, the angel's fingers digging into his flesh slightly. Kei's magic swirled toward the other man's touch, the familiar warmth of his fire heating his skin. His damn energy was drawn to the angel, whether Kei wanted to acknowledge it or not.

Gabe's gaze lowered to Kei's chest then back up. He cocked an eyebrow. "Are you okay? Your skin has a red tone to it."

The last thing Kei needed was for Gabriel to sense his desires. It was bad enough Kei felt Gabe's. But lying wouldn't garner him any of the angel's trust. And with the way Kei felt, he'd never be able to hide the truth. Better to give a fraction of it.

He forced a grin. "Just tired. Makes it harder to rein in my power, which seems to be drawn to you."

"A side effect of your spell. As I said...you should take more care in what tokens you inscribe on the ground. Especially when you make an offering with your blood. It often causes...complications."

"What kind of complications?"

Gabe smirked. "Rest. We'll talk once we're both stronger."

Kei frowned, glancing at the door. "You'll put up the wards?"

"I already said I would."

"Again, you don't have to be an ass about it." He relaxed into the cushions, ignoring the way his magic protested when Gabe eased back, his hands no longer touching Kei's body. Orange wisps curled along his skin in beckoning before sheer exhaustion won, and the energy sank beneath his flesh.

Kei closed his eyes, the soft sounds of Gabriel shuffling

around the room lulling him to sleep. Noises touched the edge of his consciousness, an ever-present thrum of Gabe's power keeping him from fully succumbing. It was as if the other man's energy reached out to him, an echoed pulse of it strumming beneath Kei's skin.

He drifted, immersed in darkness, the remembered feel of Gabe's lips on his—his hands tight around Kei's waist—playing in his head. He hadn't intended for the kiss to be more than a transfer of energy while providing them appropriate cover, but damn—as soon as he'd sealed his mouth to Gabe's... His magic had surged to life, stiffening his cock against his jeans in the process, narrowing every thought to the soft play of flesh on flesh.

He'd given into the urge to palm Gabe's back, run his hands the length of the man's spine until he'd grazed his wings. God, Kei hadn't expected them to be so soft—like velvet only living. Gabe had tensed instantly, and Kei had been about to lower his fingers when the man had moaned and drawn Kei closer. As if he couldn't quite stop himself, either.

Kei inhaled as he opened his eyes, blinking back the fuzziness as he willed his heart to calm. Shit, just thinking about the encounter quickened his pulse and roughened his breathing. And he had no idea what to do about it.

He levered up, swinging his legs off the couch as he braced his elbow on the arm. The room swam for a moment then settled, the soft whisper of breath drawing his attention. He glanced to his right, exhaling as he stared at Gabriel. The man reclined in the armchair across from Kei, Gabe's massive body making the furniture look small. His eyes were closed—the dark cast of his eyelashes a stark contrast to the creamy white of his skin. The man still hadn't put on a shirt, his flesh gleaming in the splash of moonlight filtering through the windows. Odd shadows reflected across his chest, the familiar silhouette gaining Kei's attention.

He turned, staring at the sigils drawn on the glass. Shit, Gabe hadn't been kidding. He'd more than secured the room. Hell, Kei wasn't sure he even knew what some of the symbols meant.

You should take more care in what tokens you inscribe on the ground. Especially when you make an offering with your blood. It often causes...complications.

He didn't have a clue what Gabe was referring to. Though, the fact Kei felt an echoed strum inside his chest suggested his connection to the angelic man was increasing. Becoming a living entity within Kei.

He returned his gaze to Gabriel. The man's muscles flexed as he twitched, his head rolling over to one side. A ghosted flash of his wings wavered against the cloth, making Gabe appear every inch the powerful being he claimed to be, before fading. Seems the man's glamour was wavering in strength, Kei just didn't know if it was because Gabe was sleeping or because he wasn't recharging the way he should.

Fuck, Kei still couldn't believe the man was an archangel. Or why he'd shown up in place of the soulless beast Kei had attempted to conjure. Nothing made sense.

He scrubbed his hand down his face. Archangel or not, it was a fundamental fuck up. And unless Gabe decided to help him, Kei was back where he started, only worse. It'd take more than a couple of days to regain his strength—and that was if they didn't run into any problems. If

Abaddon had sensed Kei's spell and sent more demons after him...

There's no us once I regain my strength.

Just his luck. He'd summoned an angel who couldn't stand humanity.

"Archangel."

Kei snapped his head toward Gabe, instantly drawn to those damn eyes. The man was more than dangerous.

Gabriel frowned. "And I have no grievance with humanity. Not when I'm sent here as an ambassador. It's being plucked from my home against my wishes that I don't like."

Kei stared at him, a cold shiver working down his spine. "How did you..." He inhaled sharply. "You're spying on my thoughts, now?"

Gabe cocked his head to the side. "I didn't spy. You practically screamed it inside my head."

"Inside... You can hear what I'm thinking without messing with my mind?"

The muscle in Gabe's jaw jumped. "I warned you about using sigils you weren't familiar with. That there'd be...consequences."

"You also decided not to tell me about those consequences when I asked."

He snorted. "You were barely conscious. I doubt you'd have remembered."

Kei let his head fall back against the couch. "So it's your power I feel strumming beneath my skin? Your thoughts that play in a loop inside my mind?"

"You say it like you're the only one affected. I didn't ask to have your feelings merge with mine."

"Could this get any worse?" Kei pressed his head

against the cloth. "More than conscious, now. So feel free to start talking."

Gabriel stared at him for a few moments, his brow furrowing as he exhaled. "You're still weak."

"So are you." Kei scoffed at Gabe's frown. "Please, your damn wings were flickering in and out when I first woke up. Your glamour could use some work."

"Did it occur to you that perhaps I was conserving my power?"

"If you were, then why didn't you just scrap the damn mirage altogether? It's just us here, and I already know who and what you are."

"Because it's not that simple. I'm not..." He sighed, looking as if he wanted to say more, before shaking his head. "Do you always have to argue?"

"Guess you just bring out the best in me, buddy." Kei raked a hand through his hair. "Sorry. It's been one hell of a night. Now about those consequences?"

Gabe clenched his jaw, again, looking as if chatting was the last thing on his mind. "You said you'd expected to get a blood demon...to possess. How, exactly, did you think you'd accomplish that?"

"The old fashioned way. I was going to cast another spell once it'd appeared. Like I said...all I needed was a vessel."

"A *worthy* vessel." Gabe arched a brow. "Words have meaning, Kei. Every word."

"I know that. I'm not stupid." He pursed his lips. "Are you telling me I got you because you're the only worthy vessel for me?"

"Don't be ridiculous. Your spell shouldn't have dragged me down here. It's more that you get the most worthy entity that's within your summoning power. Which means you were never guaranteed a blood demon."

"Even if that's true—"

"It's true."

"Fine. You're the master of fucking symbols. So answer me this, Einstein, why did I get you?"

"I don't know. But there are other...issues."

"Besides getting a pain in the ass angel?"

Gabe glared at him, and Kei held back a smile. He didn't know why he enjoyed sparring with the man as much as he did, but be damned if he'd stop now. Not when he felt so on edge. Torn between wanting to punch the guy in the face for the smug smile curving his lips or claim his mouth again.

Gabe sighed, and Kei cursed under his breath. Great, the bastard had probably heard his damn thoughts.

He gazed at Gabe. "You can sigh all you want, but it's not just my head that's replaying that kiss."

Gabe's cheeks reddened slightly. "No, but it was your spell that bound us together."

Kei leaned forward. "Bound us? What the hell does that mean?"

"It means that some of those symbols were binding sigils. And seeing as you used your blood to feed the spell..."

"It bound us together? Are you serious?"

"Do you honestly think I'd lie about something that important?"

"No, but...fuck."

Kei pushed to his feet, taking a few shaky steps away, unsure if the dizzy feeling in his head was from lack of power or the words still ringing inside his mind. Bound.

By blood. Though he didn't quite understand the extent of their connection, the obvious symptoms were enough to convince him he'd more than fucked up.

Gabe chuckled. "Perhaps you should be grateful you got me by accident. Being bound to a blood demon…"

Kei glared at him over his shoulder. "Trust me. From where I'm standing it's a tossup."

Gabe merely shrugged as he tapped his head. "To answer your question…it means I know when you're lying."

Kei flipped him the bird, leaning on the couch as the room swam. Black dots played at the edges of his vision, a warm feeling slowly billowing up his torso. Strong hands grabbed his shoulders a moment before he was tugged against a wall of male flesh, the hard press of lean muscles clearing his head slightly. He focused on Gabe, wishing he could shove the guy away without falling on his ass.

Gabe gave him a shake of his head. "You are stubborn, even for a mage. You need to rest."

"Not until you tell me everything you know."

"I have."

Kei scoffed. "You haven't told me shit other than that we're bound." He squinted as the room flip-flopped again. "For how long?"

"Let's get you on lying down again before you pass out on the floor, and I leave you there."

Kei moved with him the few steps back, once again sinking into the cushions. "Answer the question, Gabriel. How long are we bound?"

Gabriel eased away, staring at him as if he'd never seen a human before. "Does it matter?"

"Of course, it matters."

"Until you either send me back, or…"

Kei frowned when he didn't continue. "Or…"

Gabe drew himself up, once again looking every inch the warrior Kei suspected hid beneath the pale skin and pure beauty. "Or until this quest of yours is over. One way or another."

"As in alive or dead."

Gabe's lips quirked. "You're a mage. You know better than anyone that killing the sorcerer usually ends their spell."

"Does that mean I should watch my back? Lest you stick a knife in it?"

Gabe sighed, moving over to the chair. His wings flickered again before the man's shoulders sank and a burst of creamy feathers fluttered to life behind him. Sweat beaded his brow as he raised his gaze to Kei's. "I'm many things—have killed more than my fair share of humans and demons alike—all in the name of peace. But even I have lines I won't cross."

"Here's hoping I'm one of those lines."

"You're…unexpected. Now rest. And once you're stronger, you'll tell me everything you know about Abaddon and his mission."

Kei sighed, allowing his eyelids to drift shut. He wasn't the only one who was unexpected. He just hoped Gabriel was willing to do more than merely listen to his story. Kei needed an ally. Hell, he needed a miracle.

CHAPTER FOUR

Gabriel sat across from Kei, watching as the man faded back to sleep. Passed out, if Gabriel were being honest. How the sorcerer had managed to even stand was a mystery. Not when Gabriel felt his exhaustion. The few hours obviously hadn't recharged the mage.

Gabriel glanced over his shoulders, staring as his feathers rustled against the cloth. Kei wasn't the only one who didn't seem to be recovering. Despite the energy the sorcerer had given him, Gabriel had gotten to the point where simply holding his glamour took more power than he cared to admit. A fact Kei had picked up on.

Gabriel let his head fall into his hands. He hated that he didn't know how he'd gotten there. How Kei had managed to summon him. What he'd told the sorcerer was true. Kei's spell could have snared him, but only if he'd already been within its reach. And seeing as Gabriel's last memory was that of his home, he shouldn't have been close enough to be an option.

Doubts teased the edge of his mind. Pieces of a puzzle

that didn't quite fit together. He tried to recall the markings Kei had inscribed. Surely there was something he'd missed within them? A reason he'd been plucked from Heaven. Unless...

He stilled. What if Kei had performed a different version of the blood spell? One far more powerful. After all, Gabriel had overlooked one aspect of the incident. If he was Kei's worthy vessel that meant the mage was Gabriel's. Which, in turn, meant their connection was far more complicated than a simple summoning.

Gabriel groaned. He was too weak to work through every possibility. Especially ones he didn't want to consider. He lifted his head enough to focus on his hands, allowing a bit of his power to surge to the surface—put his weakness to the test. Golden light colored his skin, merging into a brilliant white as a shimmering ball rose above his palms, flickering to the beat of his heart.

Sweat beaded his brow, the sheer strength required to keep the light above his hands fading his vision at the edges. He clenched his jaw, willing the orb to increase before allowing it to shatter into a blaze of blinding rays. Pain tightened his chest, his breath loud in the still room.

Gabriel sucked in a few ragged gasps, relaxing as the pounding beneath his ribs eased, his pulse slowly returning to normal. He'd never experienced this kind of weakness before. Had to concentrate just to hold a glamour or channel a stream of light. Though it hadn't been that long, his power should be increasing. Gradually filling the hole inside his chest—the one that nagged at him that this was more than an accidental summoning. He'd been on Earth before, and granted it'd been a few centuries, but his powers had always been absolute. While he'd contest he wasn't quite the warrior Michael was, he'd certainly never shied away from his responsibilities. His battles. But now... He wouldn't be much use to anyone if he couldn't so much as mask his identity. At this rate, he'd be lucky just to stand up.

He closed his eyes. He could sort out the issues once he'd gotten some rest. Given his grace time to adjust to being bound to Kei and this place. With any luck, he'd be back to full strength by morning. Of course, that meant he'd have to decide on how they'd proceed. Carrying out a mission he'd been given was one thing. Helping a sorcerer he didn't even know kill his former brother...

Abaddon. Gabriel hadn't thought he'd ever hear that name again. Not after watching the man cast himself out of Heaven. Choose a path far darker than any had foreseen. If there was even a chance the fallen angel was alive—was involved in a scheme to destroy the Earth...

He pushed aside the thoughts. Surely, he'd have been sent here on a mission if that kind of evil was underfoot. Either way, he needed to rest. The steady whisper of Kei's breath calmed the nervous fluttering in Gabriel's stomach —the man's echoed heartbeat lulling Gabriel to sleep. Images teased his consciousness—hands gripping his shoulders, the sound of wings beating against his skin. A hint of brimstone suffused the air as pain arced across his flesh. He stiffened, the sudden sensation of falling tightening his gut. He reached for something to grasp, fisting his hands around something firm as the sensation ripped through his body. A voice rasped nearby, the familiar tone tugging at him.

"Damn it, Gabriel, wake up!"

Gabriel bolted forward, his chest heaving, the frantic

draw of his breath filling the room. He blinked, finally focusing on Kei. The man hovered several inches away, brow furrowed, green eyes dark with concern.

He frowned, glancing at Gabriel's hands before nodding. "You okay?"

Gabriel stared at the man, wondering why his fingers hurt so much only to realize he'd clamped his hands around Kei's forearms—his fingertips digging hard into the other man's flesh. He willed himself to let go but barely managed to loosen his hold.

Kei's mouth lifted into a smile. "Figure that must have been some dream."

Gabriel snapped his gaze up. "Dream?"

"Nightmare more like it. You were screaming and making the damn room shake. Looks like your power's in there somewhere. Your skin was glowing until you grabbed me when I tried to wake you. That's when it winked out."

Gabriel glanced at his hands again. Why couldn't he simply release Kei?

Kei sighed. "Can't imagine this is easy, even for an archangel. You might want to cut yourself some slack, especially if we really are bound to each other." He eased back slightly, but not to the point he pulled free of Gabriel's hold. "You're not the only one feeling... unsettled. Though, I suggest trying to rein in that power of yours. Even with the sigils you inscribed, it's like a bloody beacon. And I'm betting Abaddon can sense your energy."

"I sealed the room. Nothing should get in or out."

"I trust you, it's just...until we figure out how, exactly, you got here, it might be best not to assume anything.

Besides, you don't look near strong enough to be wasting any energy. So pull it back."

Gabriel pursed his lips. He didn't want to confess he didn't know how to pull it back. That control had always been a given and being like this—reckless—was completely foreign.

Kei's fingers grazed over his skin, the warm brush of flesh jerking Gabriel out of his thoughts. He focused on Kei, noting the way his full lips twitched into a slight grin.

Kei arched a brow. "I'll ask you again, are you okay?"

Gabriel opened his mouth to answer, but nothing more than a throaty moan managed to form on his tongue. Memories of Kei's lips pressed against his, the man's hands on his body, wove through Gabriel, making the room suddenly hot.

Kei's grin widened, a low chuckle breezing across Gabriel's chin. The mage leaned in, stopping with his mouth just grazing Gabriel's. "Tell me something, Gabriel. Is this fixation solely due to the spell? Is that the only reason you feel anything for me?"

Gabriel swallowed, nearly choking at the dry rasp in his throat. He drew a quick gasp, cursing the mix of Kei's breath that seemed to fill him. "I don't—"

"Careful, buddy. I can sense your thoughts, too, remember? Might be best not to lie directly to my face."

He clenched his jaw, fighting the urge to close the last bit of distance. Taste Kei's mouth without it being a transfer of energy. "It's not just the spell. But you already know that if you're truly inside my mind."

Kei beamed. "I do. But damn if I didn't want to hear you admit it before I did this..."

Kei dipped forward, sealing his lips to Gabriel's,

coaxing him to open his mouth. Gabriel complied, humming as Kei's tongue swept inside, brushing the length of his. Warm, spicy essence filled his senses, the distinct flavor of Kei's scent wrapping around Gabriel. He tightened his hold on the other man's arms, dragging him closer, wanting to feel the sorcerer's chest pressed against his. The firm ridge of his cock nestled against his groin.

Kei moved with him, going to his knees as he freed one arm, sliding his hand behind Gabriel's neck—cupping his head as he threaded his fingers in Gabriel's hair—effectively deepening the kiss. Gabriel shuffled forward, tugging Kei against him as he snaked his hand around the man's waist, palming the small of his back. Firm muscles flexed beneath his fingers, the hidden strength only increasing the need burning through his core.

Kei released him, moving his mouth to Gabriel's neck. Light nips peppered his skin as the other man slowly descended, kissing his way along Gabriel's shoulder.

Kei hummed against Gabriel's flesh. "I'm not sure if it's because you're so damn pure or because there's a dose of sin mixed in, but shit..." He eased back slightly. "You make me want to put that question to the test."

He glanced behind Gabriel, arching a brow as he released Gabriel's head then smoothed his fingers along Gabriel's back, teasing the edge of his wings. His breath caught as fire shot down his spine, coiling dangerously tight in his sac. Shit, another few passes and he just might come in his pants.

Kei's smile turned wicked. "So that does turn you on. Wasn't sure if I'd imagined it before. Makes me wonder how you'd react if I ran my fingers along the entire length of your wings and back." He closed in, his lips brushing across Gabriel's. "How many other lovers have done that to you?"

His breath hitched again at the man's question.

Kei shook his head. "Speechless? Any other time, I'd find that appealing, but... Tell me, Gabriel. How many other lovers have made you hard by touching your wings?"

"I'm an archangel."

"So?" He licked the seam of Gabriel's lips. "Does that mean you haven't had any encounters? No pleasures of the flesh and all that?"

"I've...experienced pleasure. Just not in the form you're suggesting."

"So, you're saying I'm the first. Sin or not, I love the thought of that." He scratched his nails along Gabriel's wing. "Not at all what I expected. So damn soft, but... alive. Like an extension of you."

Gabriel shivered as heat spiraled along his skin, drawing his power to the surface. It glowed beneath his flesh, increasing in strength at the answering crimson hue of Kei's magic. His numbing weakness faded into the background as his energy melded with Kei's, the strumming force stealing his breath.

Kei inhaled, his breath tickling Gabriel's neck. "Damn. Never had that happen before. What is it about you that gets under my skin? Calls to me on a level I've never felt before? Is this because we're bound to each other?"

Gabriel moistened his lips, cursing inwardly when his tongue brushed across Kei's soft flesh. "Being bound plays a part, but..."

Kei arched a brow. "But?"

"Nothing that I saw in the sigil explains the extent we seem to be...affecting each other."

Kei smiled. "Good. Wouldn't want this to be nothing more than some fucked up marks on the ground. Not that I have a clue what this is, exactly. But my gut's telling me you're worth being my biggest mistake."

Kei slanted his mouth over Gabriel's again, this kiss more urgent than the last. As if the other man had been holding back before. Their energy merged, flickering tiny flames across Kei's skin, the red light licking at Gabriel's flesh. Kei moaned, shifting his hands into a tighter hold, when the door behind the other man shook.

Kei pulled back, glancing at the entrance before looking at Gabriel. "Did you do that?"

"Why would I shake the door?"

"You shook it in your sleep. Thinking you don't really have the control you think you do."

"I was asleep. Besides, I'm not the only one who's had trouble controlling their power."

"Maybe not, but..." Kei stiffened a moment before his magic flared, filling the room with a sudden blast of light. He grabbed Gabriel, shoving him to the floor. "Get down."

His words lit the air a second before the door shook again, then flew open, an echoed bang ringing through the room. Gabriel looked up as three men walked through the smoking entrance, cocky grins gracing their faces. They stopped, their gazes landing on him.

Kei muttered under his breath, cupping Gabriel's shoulder. "Shit. Stay down."

Gabriel grabbed his hand. "Kei..."

Kei gave him a guarded smile. "Nothing I can't handle, just...keep out of the line of fire."

Kei pushed to his feet, and Gabriel didn't miss the slight sway before he braced his legs apart and crossed his arms over his chest. His magic seemed to vibrate just below his skin, casting a red hue along his flesh.

He released a weary sigh. "Balkie. And here I thought I'd locked your ass up in that warehouse."

A blond man stepped forward, his harsh features lifting into a wide grin. "Did you really think that devil's trap would hold me forever, Kei?"

"Can't blame me for hoping. How'd you get out?"

Balkie shrugged. "I had help."

"Help? Didn't realize demons understood the concept. Thought you were only loyal to yourself."

"That's generally the case...except when it comes to you." He took a few steps inside, glancing around the room before settling his gaze on Kei, again. "You, my friend, are a wanted commodity. A loose end Abaddon isn't willing to simply let wander about, causing all sorts of problems. Our master wants you dead. And he's going to some pretty extreme lengths to accomplish that."

"Like breaking my sigils?"

"Please. Did you really think it couldn't be broken? Though I have to say, the ones you used here..." He chuckled. "They're old school. Very powerful. Took a lot more than erasing part of the seal to get inside. Which makes me think I'm not the only one who's had help."

Balkie's focus dropped to Gabriel, the man's eyes burning black for a few moments before shifting back. "Looks like you've got a new friend. What's his name?"

"He's none of your concern. Now, why don't we cut with the pleasantries and get down to why you're here.

You only brought a couple of men with you. That won't be enough to kill me."

"Usually, no. But I saw that little summoning you left in the graveyard. Quite the offering you made. The kind you don't bounce back from quickly. Betting you aren't recovered, yet."

Flames sprang to life along Kei's arms, the sheer heat from his power blasting through the room. "You betting your life on that, because I won't simply trap you this time."

Balkie's smile faltered as he took a step back. "Nice show, but even I can tell you're weak."

"Am I?"

A stream of light shot out from Kei's palm, striking the man on Balkie's right. The guy screamed as the red hue consumed his body, exploding it a shower of ash.

Balkie tsked. "Is that all you've got? Hell, Tanner will be back in another body before we're finished. All you did was draw this out."

Kei grinned. "That was just a warning shot. Trust me, you won't be coming back."

"And why's that? Because of your friend?" The man laughed, the mechanical sound grating along Gabriel's nerves. "Sorry, Kei, but you're not the only one who has an angel in their pocket. The only difference is that mine still has his power. Speaking of which...you're not the reason we're here." He pointed at Gabriel. "We want him. Hand him over, and we'll leave. Let you get some rest before we pay you another visit. Besides, you know Abaddon wants the privilege of killing you himself."

Kei's gaze snagged Gabriel's for a moment before Kei stepped in front of him when Gabriel gained his feet.

"He's not going anywhere, least of all with you. Now, I suggest you leave while you have the chance."

"He's not worth dying over. Bastard can't even help you—not now. His brother saw to that. He's nothing but a burden. A shell of what he once was. So play it smart. Give Gabriel to us, and we'll leave."

Kei tensed at the mention of Gabriel's name.

Balkie laughed. "Didn't think I knew who he was, did you? Funny, after all your battles with Abaddon, I didn't think you'd go for another angel. Especially a fallen one. But then you mages aren't exactly known for your smart choices."

Kei's magic flickered then steadied, his expression masking any emotion. "Like I said, Gabe's not going anywhere with you. So I suggest you leave before you find out just how powerful my new friend is."

"Exactly how much of your blood did you sacrifice in that summoning? Or are you choosing not to hear the parts you don't like. The angel can't help you. He's lost his damn grace." Balkie grinned. "Oh, fuck. You didn't know, did you? You think he's just weakened from the experience. Get a grip, Kei. Archangels don't need to recover. They're all powerful. Heaven's greatest weapons and all that bullshit. Your friend's out of juice—for good." He moved forward again. "So give him up. He'll only slow you down."

Kei clenched his jaw, the muscles in his back flexing. "You're bluffing. You're a demon. You don't know shit about angels. Less about his kind."

"I know what Abaddon told me. When are you going to get it through that thick skull of yours that there's far more at work here than banishing a mage? There's a master plan, and having an arsenal of warriors ready to rain down vengeance from above isn't part of that. Now, give us the angel or you can both die."

Kei stuck out his arm, stopping Gabriel when he stepped beside him. Kei shook his head. "You want Gabriel? You'd better hope you can kill me because that's the only way you'll get remotely close to him." The flames kissing his skin flared higher, glaring light through the room. "Your choice, demon."

Gabe huffed. While a part of him was touched that the sorcerer was standing up for him, it certainly didn't sit well with his sense of pride. He was considered one of Heaven's greatest weapons—had dealt out more than his fair share of justice. He didn't need protecting. He nudged Kei. "Kei, I don't need—"

Kei stopped him with a pointed look, his thoughts more than clear. Kei wasn't asking. The mage looked at Balkie, motioning to the door. "Well?"

Balkie sneered, eyes burning into black again as two chairs off to his left shook, then soared toward them. Kei barely shifted his gaze as fire engulfed the wooden frames, shattering flaming splinters through the air. Kei's table appeared through the billowing smoke and ash, the thick surface reflecting the orange firelight.

Kei raised his hands as he moved in front of Gabriel, splitting the table in half around them with a single finger of light. Shards pelted Gabriel's skin as the pieces whooshed past, crashing into the wall behind them. Kei shifted, targeting the two demons standing near the door, sending a wall of fire toward them. Balkie growled, countering Kei's attack. The flames hissed when they impacted an invisible bubble, shooting upwards before winking out.

Kei grunted, leaning forward before being flung across the room, his body crashing against the wall. He fell to the floor, a muted groan drifting through the air.

Balkie snickered. "Guess you should have thought about the consequences of using that much energy in your summoning. Pretty damn stupid to leave yourself vulnerable like this, especially for an angel who can't even help defend you. All that display of magic, and I still won." He focused on Gabriel. "Looks like your time's run out, Gabriel."

Gabriel firmed his stance, allowing his power to shimmer across his skin. "I suggest you leave before I send you somewhere even Lucifer won't be able to find you."

"You might want to save some of that power. Though, seeing as you'll be dead in a few moments, it probably doesn't matter."

Balkie snarled, extending his hands as ghostly fingers settled around Gabriel's throat, the icy feel stealing his breath. Numbing pain erupted in his skull, blurring his vision and spinning the room. He increased his energy, determined to break the demon's hold, when a flash of light filled the room.

Balkie screamed, the hands around Gabriel's neck falling away. He blinked back the fuzziness, watching as the two demons writhed within a strange orange light, their bodies convulsing before collapsing on the ground, their dark essence escaping out the door. He turned. Kei knelt near the wall, lips moving, his voice just discernible above the hissing fire.

Gabriel rushed over to the man, catching him as he dropped to his knees, the red glow on his skin quickly fading. Gabriel brushed back the man's hair, noting the pale cast to his skin. "Kei?" He glanced down, shaking his head at the sigil inscribed on the floor with Kei's blood. "You haven't recovered near enough to perform a banishing spell of that magnitude. I told you I didn't need you to protect me."

Kei groaned, finally looking up at Gabriel before motioning to the door. "Seemed like a good idea at the time. But it won't last long, and it won't stop others from taking their place. And if I know Abaddon, he's got a small army lined up just to take you out. Shit, I don't even know how he tracked you down this fast." He wet his lips, grimacing in apparent pain. "Go. Quickly. I'll hold them off as long as I can. You need to contact whatever brothers or sisters you trust. Just...be careful. This is far more involved than I thought. If he's getting rid of Heaven's only defense..."

Gabriel's stomach dropped, the remembered feel of the demon's invisible hold sending a chill down his spine. If he'd truly lost his grace...

Kei punched him in the shoulder. "Balkie's a demon. He'll say anything to get the upper hand. I'm sure you just need some more rest. Now...go. We're out of time."

"Not without you."

"Damn it, Gabriel. You're far more important. Don't you see that? Besides, I couldn't live with myself if I let them hurt you. I..."

Gabriel shook his head when footsteps echoed outside the door.

"Shit." Kei tugged against Gabriel's hold. "Let go and step back. Then run once I clear the room, got it?"

"You're not strong—"

"I can't kill them all. Hell, odds are I won't be able to kill Abaddon, either. So take whatever chance you get. You. Michael. Whoever's left. You might be able to stop him."

Gabriel glanced at the doorway when more men crossed the threshold, stopping just inside. Their eyes gleamed black, their gazes fixed on him. Gabriel clenched his jaw, hooking one arm around Kei's waist as he heaved him upright.

"Damn it, Gabriel, I can't activate—"

"Wrap your arms around me and hold on. No matter what happens, don't let go."

Kei's eyes widened. "Gabriel?"

"Trust me. Close your eyes."

Kei spared the demons one last glance then grabbed Gabriel, muttering under his breath as he tightened his arms around Gabriel's chest. "I swear, if this kills us outright..."

Gabriel smiled. "It just might."

He hung his head, channeling all his power into a single thought. Golden light blazed through the room, the lingering echo of voices sounding around him a moment before everything blurred into white.

CHAPTER FIVE

"Shit!"

Kei's voice keened into a painful cry as the bright, white light seemed to burn through his skin. He squeezed shut his eyes, snugging his hold on Gabriel as the air around them stole Kei's breath, pressing against his chest until he thought he'd pass out. The light increased then faded, gradually releasing the pressure on his body.

He sucked in a quick gasp, blinking open his eyes. Shadows lined the walls of a small cabin, the glowing moonlight casting shapes across the floor. Gabriel sagged against him, taking him to his knee as he caught the other man's weight. Cold stone bit into his palm as he supported the angel against him, finally shifting onto his ass.

He cushioned Gabe's head, slowly easing him onto his lap. Kei stroked back the man's hair, sighing in relief when Gabe's lips twitched. "Gabe?"

The angel groaned but didn't rouse, a grimace twisting his features.

"Damn it. I told you to run…"

He blew out a slow breath. He didn't know what Gabriel had done—how he'd seemingly transported them somewhere else—but regardless, he owed the guy his life. A debt he wasn't certain he'd live long enough to repay.

The angel can't help you. He's lost his damn grace.

Kei stared at Gabriel as Balkie's words echoed inside his mind. Though what he'd told Gabe was true—demons would say anything to try and gain the upper hand—Kei couldn't shake the feeling that Balkie might have been right. Gabriel losing his grace explained more than Kei cared to admit. Starting with why the man wasn't regaining his strength.

Kei's skin prickled, the remnants of Gabe's energy still tingling beneath Kei's flesh. Fallen or not, the other man had displayed more than a strong show of power. He'd been epic. Like the archangels of lore. And Kei was pretty damn sure whatever trick Gabe had used to transport them had also disposed of the demons, their anguished screams still playing in Kei's head.

He sighed, giving into the urge to trace the strong line of Gabe's jaw—brush his thumb along the other man's lips. Kei didn't know when he'd decided kissing the angel was a good idea, but damn if he could stop himself. And if it hadn't been for Balkie, Kei would have taken it much further—as far as Gabe would have let him. Finally quench the burning need coiled inside Kei's gut. Or at least, temper it. Somehow, he doubted making love to Gabe once would quench anything. In fact, Kei had a pretty good idea it'd only increase his desire. Make him want things he knew he couldn't have.

"Bloody hell."

Just his luck. His first attraction in what felt like forever, and it was for an angel. And not just any angel. Gabriel. Archangel and ultimate messenger of Heaven. Kei was definitely crazy.

No, he was cursed.

He chuckled at the thought. If having Gabriel bound to him was a curse, Kei wasn't sure he wanted to find the cure. There was something dangerously right about the way they affected each other. As if the connection went soul deep.

He sighed. He'd stopped worrying about his soul years ago—when he'd all but sold it for what he thought was the greater good. Fuck, he'd been naive. Choosing to see what he'd needed to instead of what was actually happening. Believing the lies when his gut had told him otherwise.

He scrubbed a hand down his face. He'd paid for his mistakes. Abaddon had seen to that. Hell, Kei was still paying, and he had a bad feeling his debt wouldn't end until he'd given his life.

He gazed down at Gabriel when the man groaned again, shifting Gabe in his lap slightly. Pain creased Gabe's forehead, another grimace shaping his lips. Kei smoothed his finger along the angel's cheek, smiling when he eased. Kei would have to find a way to ensure the other man didn't die alongside of him. Not when it seemed Gabriel had already lost so much. God, Kei hoped Balkie was wrong. That the spell was the reason behind Gabe's continued fatigue. That given enough time...

Not that they had time. Though Kei had no idea where Gabe had transported them to, he had no doubt Abaddon would source out their location soon enough. That they'd face an endless stream of demons until they'd either won or died trying. Christ. This was far more than Kei had bargained for. Though, if he was going to die...

He traced his finger down Gabe's neck, across his shoulder to the edge of one wing. Kei wasn't quite sure when he'd developed a fetish for feathers, but damn if the velvety feel of Gabe's wings didn't turn him on. And knowing he was the first man to touch them intimately...

Kei swallowed against the rush of need that burned through his veins. Now that the immediate danger had passed, his dick had seized control again, filling his head with images of Gabe spread out before him. Naked. Aroused. The angel's body was massive, and Kei already knew the man's cock matched the rest of him, though seeing it and feeling it were distinctly different. And Kei hadn't felt near enough of Gabe. He wanted to feel the man's tightly wound muscles flex beneath him. See firsthand how hard Gabe's cock got when Kei took it in his mouth. Savor the smooth glide of Gabe's skin as he moved above him.

But he didn't just want to fuck Gabe. He wanted to consume the man. Learn every dip and angle, memorize every plane. Then have Gabe do the same to him. Feel him move within Kei's body. Give as much as he took. Hell, give everything.

His damn shaft jerked against his stomach, pressing painfully against the zipper of his jeans. Why he had such little control, where the angel was concerned, mystified Kei. But he was done fighting it. Now that he knew Gabe felt something for him—however transient it might be— Kei wasn't going to waste time reining in his desire. Not when he could spend it lost in Gabe's body. Surrounded by the other man's scent, the hard press of his muscles.

Gabe stirred within his arms, eyelids slowly blinking open. That bright blue gaze snagged his, and Kei couldn't help but smile as he returned his hand to the man's face, gently cupping his jaw.

He shook his head. "And you called me reckless."

Gabe tensed as he glanced at their surroundings, finally easing in Kei's grasp. "I don't recall saying that word."

"Not exactly. It was implied. So...where are we?"

Gabe wet his lips, the slow sweep of his tongue across the pink flesh spiking another jolt of need through Kei's gut. "Sanctuary."

Kei snorted. "Are all angels this evasive? Where's this sanctuary?"

Gabe frowned. "Does it matter?"

"There a reason you can't tell me?" Kei groaned. "Shit. You didn't take us..." He pointed at the ceiling. "Upstairs, did you? I was only joking about that miraculous act of yours killing us."

"We're not dead. Do all sorcerers have such little faith?"

"Only the smart ones."

Gabe released a weary breath, allowing Kei to help him sit up. "It's a small cabin close to a church I frequented during previous missions to Earth. A place Abaddon isn't aware of. In case you haven't noticed, archangels aren't exactly social creatures. We crave solitude, even when tasked with orders. So, back in the beginning, we all claimed a place where we could meditate. This was mine."

He smiled as he surveyed the room. "We should be safe... for a while."

"I'll take whatever we can get." Kei nudged the other man. "Thanks. Not sure how you mustered enough power to achieve..." he waved at the cabin, "...this. But... Guess I owe you, now."

Gabe arched a brow. "I wouldn't thank me. Half of that energy was most likely yours. Your magic seems to have a penchant for fueling me."

"I'll try to remember that." Kei sighed. "How do you feel?"

The smile fell from Gabe's lips, his unrest suddenly palpable. He pushed to his feet then took a few shaky steps away, bracing his weight on one of the cabin's walls. Shame hunched his shoulders as he drew a ragged breath, finally glancing back at Kei. "I fell."

Kei's stomach tensed, the overwhelming pain in Gabe's voice taking Kei to his feet. He moved over to the man, getting as close as he could without touching Gabe. "You didn't fall—"

"You heard that demon. Despite what you said before, we both know he spoke the truth." Gabe looked Kei directly in the eyes. "I know you can feel it just as surely as I can. My grace...it's gone."

"No, it's not." Kei held up his hand, preventing Gabe from interrupting him. "Granted, it's... suppressed. Restrained, perhaps. And you seem to have a hard time gaining your strength, but shit, Gabe... You just transported us God knows how far. Killed those demons in the process. Hell, I can feel your damn power strumming inside me. Like an echoed heartbeat."

"It's not the same. That demon was right. I shouldn't need to recharge. My power should be absolute."

"The spell—"

"Bound me to you. Brought me here, somehow. But it doesn't explain..." He waved his hand down the length of his body as his wings fluttered against the wall. "This. I can't even hold a glamour."

"Gabriel..."

He turned, leaning fully against the wall as his head bowed to his chest. "It explains how your spell summoned me. If I were already on my way to Earth..." A shudder shook through him. "You most likely saved my life. Prevented the inevitable death from being cast out."

"How many angels survive...falling?"

Gabe raked a hand through his hair. "Very few. And those that do spend their time eking out a mostly human existence."

"Mostly human? What the hell does that mean?"

"It means that a fallen angel will retain a handful of... abilities. Most are superficial. But the worst is sensing their power without being able to channel it. Like an endless itch you can never scratch. It also marks you as a beacon to those who'd like nothing more than to prey on your wounded soul."

"Do they get to keep their wings? Because I'd have thought those would be the first to go."

"It depends on how they fall. Your spell trapped me before I completed the journey. That changes the nature of my infliction. Or maybe it's just another form of torture. A constant reminder of what I once was. I really don't know. Haven't talked to any of the fallen."

Kei stepped into Gabe's personal space, getting within

a few inches of him. "If you were cast out, it's not because of anything you did."

Gabriel glared at him, but Kei merely shook his head.

"You heard Balkie. This is so much bigger than I thought. Abaddon is part of what happened to you. From the sounds of it, he's getting rid of any threat. And we both know archangels are at the top of that list." He released a soft breath. "Which means Michael and the others are in danger. Can you contact them?"

"Normally, yes. But ever since I arrived, that avenue has been...blocked. But even if I could, using my power in that fashion would broadcast our location to every angel. Even fallen ones if they still breathe."

Kei bowed his head slightly. "So Abaddon would know where you took us."

Gabriel merely nodded. "Not that I'm convinced I could contact Michael either way. With my limited resources..."

"You just kicked major ass. I'll put my faith in you and your *limited resources* any day. But you've got a point. Neither of us is strong enough for another showdown. We need a couple of days to regroup. Recharge. Try to figure out what move to make next. Which means we need to safeguard this cabin."

Gabe frowned. "That demon found us regardless of the sigils I'd inscribed."

"That's because it wasn't Balkie who located you."

"Then who?"

Kei pursed his lips, knowing the other man wasn't going to like what he had to say. "Do you really think it was Abaddon who was behind your fall from grace? That he was able to cast you out of Heaven?"

A red flush rose in Gabe's cheeks, the blue of his eyes darkening. "I already told you. Only God or another archangel could cast..."

Kei cursed under his breath as Gabe's voice faded off, understanding dawning in the angel's eyes. Kei eased closer, pressing his chest against Gabe's. "I know this can't be easy, but...one of your brothers is part of this. We need to protect ourselves from everyone—demons and angels—until we know who we can and can't trust." He sighed when Gabe simply stood there, staring blankly at some spot over Kei's left shoulder. "Gabriel...'

"Michael would never abandon his faith. Ever."

"Then we do everything we can to contact Michael. Or find him. But for now...we need time. I know we don't have much of that, but an archangel with limited powers and a drained mage aren't going to be a match for the forces Abaddon will send our way if he finds us, let alone actually facing him. For all we know, he's found a way to keep Michael from interfering. We have to assume we're on our own."

Gabe glanced at the windows, his expression falling flat. "I'll inscribe the necessary sigils." He sighed when Kei arched his brow. "For both demons and angels. Trust me, nothing will get inside unless we welcome it through the door."

Kei shifted enough to let Gabriel shuffle past. He palmed the man's shoulder, gently cupping it as the angel glanced back at him. "I'll find a way to fix this. I promise. No matter what it takes, I'll send you back."

Gabriel gave him a small smile. "While I appreciate both your conviction and optimism, once an angel falls, no matter the circumstances..." He turned away.

Kei leaned against the wall, watching Gabriel work, cursing when the man used his own blood to draw the marks on the windows and doors. Gabe couldn't afford to weaken himself more—not when he wasn't recovering. Other than when they'd kissed... Kei grinned. Seems there was at least one way to help the angel recharge. Even if it wasn't a deliberate exchange of energy.

Kei waited until the man moved over to a small couch, collapsing on the edge as his strength seems to wane. Hell, who was Kei kidding? Gabe had been on the verge of exhaustion when he'd woken. He'd only succeeded in weakening himself more.

Kei joined him, his leg snugged up against Gabe's. Kei's magic surged beneath his skin, warming his flesh where he touched the angel. The man inhaled, his gaze snapping to Kei's, an answering glow coloring his body. Desire darkened his eyes, his breath noticeably rougher.

Gabe looked away, pain creasing his forehead. "I'm sure you're wishing you got your blood demon, instead of me." His shoulders drooped. "Even if I want to help you..."

Kei grazed his fingers along Gabe's chin, gently but firmly raising the man's face to his. He thumbed the corner of the other man's mouth, the soft flesh sending a spike of need through his core. "You've saved my life twice in less than a day. Thinking those are pretty damn good odds. Besides, you were the one who said I got the most worthy vessel possible." He leaned in, his breath mixing with Gabe's. "Not sure what I ever did to be worthy of you, but...I'll take it."

He slanted his lips over Gabe's, keeping the contact light. Allowing the angel time to pull back if Kei's advance was unwanted. The other man stiffened, his hands rising then fisting around Kei's shirt. Kei waited, mouths still touching, until Gabe tugged him against his chest, his grip easing as he smoothed his hands along Kei's torso.

Kei hummed his approval, reaching one hand to the back of Gabe's neck as he deepened the kiss, moaning as Gabe's flavor burst along his tongue. The sweet essence matched the man's scent—pure. Fresh. Kei lingered until his lungs burned, barely moving back as he rasped in a quick gasp.

Gabe sucked in a few breaths, his head still slightly tilted to the side. "You don't have to give me your energy." The man's voice sounded raw. Far lower than before.

Kei snorted. "Is that why you think I just did that? To give you my energy?" He smiled. "That's simply a byproduct. You know why I really kissed you, Gabriel. You can sense it the same way I sense your desire. Or is it need?"

Gabriel's Adam's apple bobbed as he swallowed, his chest pressing against Kei's with every frantic inhalation. "I'm not the angel you're expecting."

"No, you're the one I need. Now either tell me to back the fuck off, or..." He nuzzled the man's nose, quickly adding his own wards to the room—guaranteeing no one would hear them, human or otherwise. "Kiss me again."

CHAPTER SIX

Gabriel stared at Kei—his mouth grazing Kei's, the man's chest flexing against his—and wondered when he'd decided getting emotionally and physically involved with the mage was a good idea. Hadn't he told himself he didn't belong there? That he should stay distant?

But the longer Kei sat beside him, waiting, the more Gabriel's resolve seemed to vanish like his grace. He drew one last breath then closed the scant distance, molding his mouth to Kei's, allowing the man's taste to fill his senses. Hot spice wove through him, the inherent heat impossible to miss.

He closed his eyes, allowing the surge in Kei's magic to dissolve any remaining doubts. Between the spell and Gabriel's physical reaction, denying they had a connection seemed futile. A wasted battle of energy he could ill afford. And if he truly had fallen, any reasons for resisting his attraction had fallen with him.

Kei's fingers tightened in his hair, the resulting tug sending a jolt of pure lust down Gabriel's spine. Though he'd experienced pleasure in many forms, it'd never been this all-consuming. This intense. And he suspected it had far less to do with the blood spell and more to who Kei truly was.

A worthy vessel.

Perhaps it was Gabriel who'd been granted that. Who'd been saved by a spell gone wrong—by a man with more honor than most.

Kei nipped at his lip when he eased back, arching a brow. "Are you still overthinking this?"

Gabriel cursed inwardly as the man's voice slid along his nerves, igniting his power until it bathed his flesh in a warm glow.

Kei laughed. "Looks like your grace agrees with me. It knows this is right."

"My grace is gone."

"No, it's just being difficult."

He trailed his fingers along Gabriel's shoulder, teasing the edge of his wing. Gabriel's energy increased, sending a finger of light through the cabin before dimming.

Kei chuckled. "See? I think it just needs the right motivation. Either way, I'm about to kiss a path across your body. If you don't want this…"

Gabriel's breath hitched as Kei moved, his mouth following the line his finger had taken. Warm, wet flesh caressed his skin as Kei licked and nipped his way to Gabriel's shoulder then down along his chest, stopping at his nipple. The mage blew a heated breath over the small nub, tightening it further.

Kei flicked his tongue across the tip, smiling against Gabriel's flesh. "Fuck, you're responsive. And don't think I can't see how hard you are beneath the denim. I considerate it pure luck you haven't burst through the zipper."

"My shaft isn't the only one that's hard."

Kei glanced up at him, flashing a mischievous smile before taking one of Gabriel's hands and placing it against his groin. The long, stiff ridge of the sorcerer's cock pulsed into Gabriel's touch, the man's roughened intake of air making him smile.

Gabriel ran his hand the length of Kei's shaft, his smile widening when Kei grunted and rested his head on Gabriel's chest. "I can feel how much you enjoy my touch." He paused. While he had no reservations about leaping forward, he'd never experienced this form of pleasure.

Kei lifted his gaze. "First time for everything, buddy. Though, I have a feeling you'll be too far gone to worry once I get my mouth on you."

"Your mouth…"

Gabriel's voice choked into moan as Kei fisted his pants, quickly opening the button and zipper before dragging them down his legs and off. His cock sprang against his stomach, the end already shiny with his arousal.

Kei hummed, lightly running his nails up Gabriel's skin, avoiding his straining erection. "Damn, you really are massive in all ways."

"Is that a problem?"

"Hell no. Couldn't be more right if I'd planned it, myself. But that's for later. For now…" He dropped a quick kiss on Gabriel's mouth before sinking to his knees between Gabriel's thighs. "All I want you to do is enjoy."

"But what about…"

Gabriel's words died on his tongue as Kei made another pass with his fingers, this time scratching along both sides of his shaft, making his cock bob out toward the man before slapping against his stomach. A sexy grin claimed Kei's lips as he finally cupped Gabriel's erection, slowly dragging his fist from root to tip. A dot of pearly fluid beaded from the thin slit, the translucent juice gleaming in the bright moonlight.

Kei brushed his thumb across the head, swirling the slickness around Gabriel's skin. The intimate touch punched his hips forward as pleasure shot down his spine.

Kei arched a brow. "I'll assume you like that. But it's nothing compared to this."

He leaned in, flicking his tongue across the flared crown, licking away the fluid. The wet caress drew a strangled moan from deep in Gabriel's chest, and he couldn't stop from anchoring his hands in Kei's hair.

Kei seemed oblivious to the way Gabriel tugged on the strands, needing the firm grip to keep him from thrusting his shaft against Kei's mouth. The man appeared intent on torturing him, another pass of the mage's tongue only increasing Gabriel's need.

"Kei…" There was no mistaking the warning tone in Gabriel's voice.

Kei glanced up at him. "Bossy, aren't we? Though, I suppose that's simply your nature, archangel and all that. You're used to getting your way. Afraid it doesn't work that way between lovers, Gabe. And this round, I'm setting the pace." He bathed Gabriel's flared head again then pulled back. "Trust me. Waiting is half the fun."

Gabriel tightened his hold, but Kei merely chuckled, taking his time as he licked Gabriel's shaft, dipping lower to suckle his sac. Gabriel let his head fall against the back of the sofa as pleasure shot through his core. If he'd known having Kei touch him would be this intense... He clenched his jaw as a tingling sensation wove down his spine. His cock jerked in Kei's grasp, his balls pulling up painfully close.

"Breathe, buddy. I've only just started, and I've got a lot more planned before I let you explode on me."

Gabriel pried open his eyelids as he stared at the mage wedged between his thighs, Kei's hand stroking the length of Gabriel's erection. His power sent a surge of light glaring through the room, drawing a similar spike from Kei.

A stunning smile shaped the other man's lips. "Damn, you are close, aren't you? Fine. You win, but don't think I'll let you off this easy the next time." Kei leaned forward. "And there'll definitely be a next time."

Gabriel inhaled as Kei sealed his lips around Gabriel's shaft and slowly took Gabriel inside his mouth. Wet, hot flesh surrounded Gabriel's cock, the crushing pressure arching his hips off the couch. Kei placed one arm across Gabriel's lap, virtually pinning him in place as Kei paused with the head lodged at the back of his throat. The man swallowed, the resulting force making Gabriel shout Kei's name as the muscles in his abdomen strained, working to keep from spilling down Kei's throat.

Kei moaned, gradually easing back up Gabriel's length until he could release his cock. "Fuck, you're responsive. Thought you were going to come after one pass." He shook his head. "Let's see how long you can hold off."

He wedged the crown at his lips again, making a point of taking Gabriel inside an inch at a time. Immersing his flesh in liquid fire again. He unclenched one hand, moving his index finger to Kei's mouth. He traced Kei's lips, watching in fascination as his shaft reappeared covered in the other man's saliva. Kei didn't stop this time, setting up a steady rhythm that tightened Gabriel's thighs to the point he thought they'd cramp. His heavy breathing panted through the small space, Kei's name like an endless prayer from his lips.

"Kei, I can't..."

Kei increased his pace, taking Gabriel deeper as his other hand slipped beneath Gabriel's ass until a single finger teased his hole. Gabriel gasped, his breath hitching as the moist digit slowly sank past his muscles, delving deeper until it hit his prostrate.

"Dear God." Gabriel thrust forward, unable to stop himself from pistoning into Kei's mouth, matching the movement of Kei's finger inside his ass. The hot, tingly feeling in his sac billowed outwards, stealing the last of Gabriel's resolve. "Can't stop it. Kei..."

The other man only sucked harder, adding a second finger. Gabriel bowed his head toward his chest in defeat, allowing the heat in his sac to shoot forward, marking his release. He rasped Kei's name as the first jet of semen purged from the tip. Kei moaned around his cock, swallowing every spurt until Gabriel collapsed back, sweat beading his skin, his wings fluttering against the cushions of their own accord. Black teased the edges of his vision, the room fading into gray.

A muffled chuckle sounded nearby as Kei eased back on his heels, releasing Gabriel from his mouth. He dropped a kiss on Gabriel's hip, then launched forward, claiming his lips in a brutal kiss. Salty sweetness filled

Gabriel's senses, and he couldn't help but wonder if Kei would taste different.

Kei held his gaze as he moved back a few inches, their breath mixing. "Soon, you'll get to put that question to the test, but for now..." He glanced at the couch. "Guess this will have to do."

He shifted them over slightly, his hands braced on either side of Gabriel's shoulders. "You comfortable? Your wings okay?"

"I assure you. I'm not thinking about my fucking wings."

Kei's sexy grin caught him off-guard. The other man raised one hand, tracing the length of one wing, smiling as Gabriel cursed under his breath, his cock already beginning to harden. "Something tells me you might want to pay more attention to them. They get you hard as hell."

That hand finally disappeared a moment before Kei's cock brushed against Gabriel's ass, the head smearing cooling gel across the opening. Gabriel arched his brow in question.

Kei laughed. "Sorcerer. Wouldn't be very good at what I do if I couldn't lather my cock in lube with nothing more than a thought and some token words." His expression sobered slightly. "Let me know if this is too much and I'll back off. I don't want to hurt you."

"I'm an archangel."

"Who's never been fucked like this. No shame in admitting you need me to slow down."

"Any slower, and you'll find our places reversed. Just because I've never tried this, doesn't make me submissive. I suggest you remember that."

Kei leaned in, kissing his lips before resting his forehead on Gabriel's. "Fine. Maybe I need to go slower. I want to savor our time, not rut with you. You mean too much to me."

Gabriel grabbed Kei's head, pulling him down for another kiss. A fury of emotions filled his head, Kei's mixing with his until Gabriel couldn't decipher which were his. He let the thought go, losing himself in Kei's taste as the man pushed against his ass, gradually pressing inside.

Gabriel gasped, the intense pinching sensation stealing his breath. He held Kei's gaze, refusing to look away as the man slipped farther into him, pausing with only the head locked inside. Sweat beaded Kei's skin, tension shadowing his face.

Kei moved his other hand back to the sofa, bracing his weight over Gabriel. "Are you okay?"

Gabriel hissed out his breath as Kei sank deeper, claiming his ass in a slow glide. The pinching feeling faded, replaced by red-hot need. "So full." He panted out a few more breaths, grunting when Kei finally stopped, his sac slapping wetly against Gabriel's flesh. "I need..."

His head fell back, his body strung tight.

Kei kissed his jaw, gaining his attention. "What do you need?" He tsked when Gabriel merely stared at him. "Tell me, Gabriel. What do you need?"

He pressed into Kei, loving the way the man's chest covered his. "Move. I need you to move." His head fell back again. "Christ, so much."

Kei lowered himself until his body encased Gabriel's as he gradually retreated, stopping just shy of popping out before thrusting back in, locking himself fully inside. He paused, as if judging Gabriel's response, then repeated the process, adding slightly more force.

Gabriel breathed through the resulting jolts of pleasure, each upward stroke sending him higher. He smoothed his hands up Kei's chest and over his shoulders, anchoring them together as he lost himself in the steady rhythm. Kei whispered his name, dropping his mouth to Gabriel's shoulder as he shifted his hands, palming Gabriel's back. Kei's fingers dug into his skin, the firm pressure only making Gabriel want the man to move faster. Harder.

Gabriel arched into the next thrust, meeting each one with equal pressure. Their ragged breathing sounded through the room, the heady scent of sex wafting around them. Kei grunted, grabbing the edge of one of Gabriel's wings as he increased his pace again. The added stimulation pushed Gabriel higher, pooling that familiar tingly feeling in his core. He closed his eyes, knowing he was only a few more strokes away from exploding, again.

"Fuck." Kei's voice was a strangled rasp next to his ear. "Can't hold on. Too damn tight. God, you're incredible."

"Then stop holding back." Gabriel latched onto Kei's shoulder, allowing his teeth to mark the man.

"Shit. Yes!"

Kei pounded into him, all sense of control gone. The couch squeaked in protest, banging against the wall with every forceful stroke. Gabriel dug his fingers in harder, knowing he was leaving marks but too damn close to let up. Kei tightened his hold on Gabriel's wing, shouting his name before stiffening above him. Firm contractions fluttered against his flesh before Kei jerked against him, his cock emptying inside Gabriel's ass.

Gabriel moaned through his release, his shaft pulsing between them as his orgasm washed over him, stealing any remaining strength. His arms fell to his sides, his hands resting listlessly on Kei's biceps.

Kei's heavy breathing rasped in Gabriel's ear, the man's body quivering above him before relaxing onto him. Gabriel welcomed the added weight, the feel of Kei against him grounding him. This was where he belonged. Whether he recovered his grace or not—he was bound to Kei. And the spell had nothing to do with it.

Kei's muscles eased, his breathing returning to normal. He dropped a kiss on Gabriel's shoulder then pulled back, his cock still semi-hard inside him. That sexy smile tilted Kei's lips as he nipped at Gabriel's chin. "You..."

He blew out a breath as he rested his forehead on Gabriel's. "Never expected to feel so..." He hissed this time. "You okay?"

Gabriel sighed. "I thought we'd established I'm far from fragile."

Kei chuckled. "Nothing's ever straightforward with you, is it?" He brushed his lips over Gabriel's. "But I like that about you. You're...unexpected."

Gabriel moaned as Kei slipped free, instantly missing the fullness. Conflicting emotions churned in his gut as Kei stood, his gaze running up and down Gabriel's body.

The man smiled. "Shit, you're fucking beautiful."

He held out his hand, muttering some words before a cloth materialized on his palm. He dipped forward, gently cleaning Gabriel before washing himself. He muttered more words, allowing the cloth to disappear. He reached toward Gabriel. "You coming?"

Gabriel arched his brow. "Didn't we just do that?"

Kei's lips lifted into that wicked smile. "That we did. You, twice. But I meant to bed. We could both use some sleep."

"But there isn't..." Gabriel chuckled as a bed materialized in the far corner of the small cabin. "You should try to save some of that power."

"Strangest thing. Being with you makes me feel... stronger. Come to bed."

Gabriel took Kei's hand, following the man across the room. He crawled onto the mattress, smiling as a blanket settled over him once Kei had joined him. Gabriel focused his power, concentrating on creating a glamour when Kei tsked.

"I think we've established I have a thing for your feathers. So stop worrying about them and sleep. We'll talk about Abaddon and our situation tomorrow."

Gabriel glanced at Kei over his shoulder as the man snugged into him from behind, wrapping his arms around Gabriel's torso. An odd warmth spread through his chest, as his mind quieted for the first time since opening his eyes in the cemetery.

He eased into Kei's hold. "Thank you."

"Pretty sure I got as good as I gave, but...you're welcome. Sleep."

Gabriel nodded, allowing his eyelids to drift close. They could deal with Abaddon, tomorrow. Tonight belonged to Kei.

CHAPTER SEVEN

Kei hummed, blinking open his eyes. Warm light bathed the interior of the cabin, shadowed silhouettes of the sigils covering the floor. His head felt heavy, the obvious strain of the past day still tensing his shoulders. He went to roll onto his back when a large hand smoothed up his ribs and across his chest, tugging him backwards. Strong, firm muscles pressed against him, a whispered breath caressing his cheek.

"Sleep well?"

The husky rasp of Gabriel's voice sent shivers along Kei's spine, leaving a rash of goosebumps along his skin. The man's shaft poked against his buttocks, the hard length spiking a similar response.

Kei smiled, enjoying the way Gabe's fingers made lazy circles on his chest. "Like I was dead. You?"

"Not sure that's what you want to aspire to. And I haven't had much experience with sleeping. But last night was...peaceful."

"Funny, I thought you shouted my name last night."

Gabe chuckled. "I seem to recall I wasn't the only one whose voice shook the cabin." He dropped a kiss on Kei's shoulder. "I meant after. Sharing the bed with you…" He sighed, trailing one hand along Kei's ribs to his hip. "It was more than I expected."

Kei glanced at him. "More?"

"I liked feeling your heart beat against my back, then my fingertips. The way our scents seem to mix together." His exhalation skittered across Kei's shoulder. "I've never experienced that before. Hadn't realized how it'd make me feel."

Kei gave him an encouraging smile. "How's that?"

Gabe sighed. "Human."

"Gabriel…"

"I'd rather you don't lie to me just to save my feelings. I know you feel the same weakness I do."

"Weak…a bit. But I still feel your power. Your…grace. It's like a tiny heartbeat. It's not gone. Not completely, which means you should be able to get your full power back."

Gabe stared at him, a slow smile tilting half his mouth. "Thank you."

"You already thanked me last night, though like I said…got as good as I gave, buddy."

"For not losing your faith when I've clearly lost mine."

Kei placed his hand over Gabe's. "Not going to let you down."

"I'm thinking it's me who'll let you down. You need someone who can fight at your side." He huffed. "Not sure how much help I'll be."

Kei snorted. Did the man really not understand how dangerous he truly was? "You're an arch-fucking-angel.

The bloody Hand of God. Couldn't have asked for a mightier partner." He squeezed Gabe's fingers to silence him. "Just, trust me on this one. Regardless of how weak you think you are, you certainly come through in a pinch. And that's more than anyone can ask for, especially a questionable mage."

"Questionable?"

He sighed. "Do you think my past is in any way pure? I'm not much better than Abaddon."

Gabriel stiffened behind him, as his energy surged up to meet Kei's. He tsked. "I've been sharing your thoughts for nearly a day. I know the kind of man you are, Kei. And you're nothing like my brother."

"Well, he didn't target me because I'm innocent, Gabe, or because I simply got in his way. We have a past."

"You stand against him, now. That says more than whatever has occurred in your past."

"You sure about that?"

"I can feel the truth. But perhaps you're right. It's time you told me exactly how you got to that point in the cemetery in need of a blood demon."

Kei clenched his jaw. While he knew they'd have to talk about everything eventually—hell, if he'd been able to stay conscious, they would have tackled this as soon as they'd reached his place—he wasn't sure he was ready to give up the intimate connection surrounding them, now.

Gabriel chuckled, slowly stroking his fingers down along Kei's hip. "Something tells me talking isn't what you had in mind. At least, not yet."

Kei moaned as the other man fisted his cock, squeezing his length as he pumped his hand up to the tip then back. "I know we need to...fuck."

Kei moaned again as Gabriel repeated the motion, Kei's head pressing against Gabe's body. The angel nipped at his shoulder, pausing to swirl Kei's arousal around the head of his shaft.

"Agreed. That's exactly what we need to do." Gabe hummed. "Which means our chat can wait...for a bit. Especially when I can hear you begging me to taste you."

Kei's breath hitched when Gabe threaded his fingers through Kei's hair, jerking his head back. Gabe pressed onto his elbow, claiming Kei's mouth as the other man worked his fingers along Kei's cock, the rhythmic motion stealing whatever reply he'd planned.

Gabe hummed as he eased back, licking Kei's bottom lip. "Shit, but you're addictive. I knew once would never be enough. You..." He shook his head. "Guess it's time to see if I learned anything from last night."

He released his grip, rising above Kei as he went to his hands and knees. Kei reached out and stroked his fingers along the edge of Gabe's wings, smiling at the way the angel inhaled sharply, pausing long enough for Kei to trail a path all the way to the end.

Kei snorted. "Not sure what it is about your damn feathers, but fuck...can't seem to stop touching them. Or you, for that matter."

Gabe drew a deep breath, blowing it out as Kei played absently with the tip of Gabe's wing. "If I didn't know better, I'd swear you'd cast another spell on me. They've never been this sensitive."

"Maybe you just never had the right person want to touch them."

"Maybe I've never wanted anyone to touch them... until now."

Kei's lips curled into a cocky smile. "I like the sound of that even more."

Gabe shuffled over, settling between Kei's thighs. Gabe's feathers brushed against Kei's leg, sending a shiver along his spine. Gabe grinned, scratching his nails down the soft hollow below Kei's hip until he reached Kei's cock, purposely avoiding the aching length. Instead, he continued along Kei's thighs, chuckling as goosebumps rose beneath his fingers.

Gabe dipped down, blowing a heated breath across Kei's shaft. "Ever since that first kiss against the wall, I've wondered if you'd taste the same." He arched a brow. "About time I found out."

He leaned in, nuzzling Kei's crown before drawing his tongue along the head—lapping up the drops of fluid beading the tip. Kei's breath caught as heat shot along his nerves, coiling dangerously in his sac. Fuck, one pass and he was ready to come.

Gabe eased back. "Seems I'm not the only one who has issues with their control."

Kei threaded his fingers through Gabe's hair, enjoying the way the strands twisted in his grip. "Control's overrated."

Gabe laughed, licking his cock again, keeping the contact light.

Kei tugged on the other man's hair, giving him a pointed look when Gabe's gaze rose to his. "Not really in the mood to be teased, buddy. Or you'll definitely find our positions reversed, because...shit."

His words rasped into a moan as Gabe wedged Kei's shaft at his lips then slowly took him inside his mouth. Hot, wet pressure engulfed his cock as the man sucked him deep, pausing with him locked in his throat before slowly easing back.

"Christ, Gabriel. I'm not going to last a damn minute."

The other man popped free. "Then I'll assume I'm doing something right. Besides, you did say control was overrated."

He made another pass, taking Kei slightly deeper, making him clench his jaw in an attempt to stay grounded. He'd never reacted this quickly, this intensely before. And he had a dangerous feeling that it had nothing to do with their blood bond. That the damn angel had stolen his heart the moment he'd gazed at him from within the summoning circle.

Gabe looked up, then pulled away, still stroking Kei's shaft as he levered forward, his other hand landing beside Kei's shoulder as Gabe claimed his mouth. The man's tongue swept inside, tangling forcefully with Kei's until he thought his damn lungs would burst. He sucked in a quick breath when Gabe finally released him, staring down at him—the skin over his cheeks taut.

"If it's any consolation, you have far more than just my heart." Gabe released a weary breath. "You've claimed my soul. And yeah, I know it's been but a heartbeat of time in your world, but... Archangels are absolute in all they do. Justice. Mercy...love. It happens swiftly and succinctly. Whether I have my grace or not, doesn't change that."

Kei shook his head. "Knew you'd be trouble. But I guess as long as you're mine, I'm okay with that." He released one hand and traced his thumb across Gabe's lower lip. "And I'm pretty damn sure you've had my soul from the start. So shut up and make love to me, already."

He tugged Gabe's head down, claiming his mouth with

brutal intensity. Gabe allowed him a semblance of control before taking over—kissing his way back down Kei's body. The man paused at his chest, sucking at his nipple until he had to yank on Gabe's hair. Gabe ignored him, moving to the other side, making Kei's cock weep in anticipation. It wasn't until the angel had apparently satisfied his needs that he wedged himself between Kei's legs again.

He hummed, licking Kei before taking him deep. Kei pressed his head into the mattress, trying to focus on anything but the smooth, slick glide of Gabe's mouth on his flesh. On the way the other man slipped a hand beneath him, teasing his sac then moving down to his ass. Cool gel teased his skin before sinking inside. He glanced at Gabe, arching his brow.

Gabe released his cock, still pumping him as he sank his finger farther into Kei's ass. "You're not the only one with tricks. Even I have enough power to work a few feats of magic."

"You keep working that magic, and I'll come."

"Isn't that the plan? I believe I owe you at least two."

"Fuck."

"Soon. Now stop distracting me."

Gabe all but swallowed his cock as his finger eased out, pausing at the edge before plunging back in, hitting his gland as the man made another pass of his mouth. Pleasure wove down Kei's spine, his magic snapping along his skin. Tiny crimson flames arced off his body, the answering glow of Gabe's power only driving Kei higher.

Warm, white heat danced along his flesh, Gabe's energy blending with his—adding another dimension of intimacy. He'd never had a lover evoke his magic the way Gabe did. Never had it become such an all-encompassing encounter. Feeling the man on a level he hadn't realized existed outside of his spells.

Kei's magic flared, filling the room with a bright red light. Gabe's followed in kind, the colors blending into a warm orange. Their combined power kissed Kei's skin, sending a jolt of arousal down his shaft. He sighed in defeat, thrusting his hips, fucking Gabe's mouth as the man slipped another finger inside him, gently stretching his tight muscles. Kei's release pooled in his sac, and he knew he wouldn't last much longer.

He tugged on Gabe's hair. "Can't hold off. Fuck, so damn close. If you don't want me shooting this down your throat, you'd best back off."

Gabe merely met his gaze up the length of his body before closing his eyes—adding more pressure as he increased his pace. Kei huffed, knowing it would be over long before he was ready. Though, he wasn't certain he'd ever get enough. Whether Gabriel's absolute personality had rubbed off on Kei, or it was in him all along, he wasn't sure, but damn if the man hadn't gotten beneath his skin. Dared him to give everything.

Kei clenched his jaw, still pushing into Gabe's mouth, fighting the fire burning in his sac. Pleasure ripped at his restraint until there was nothing left to do but commit.

"Yes! Fuck, Gabriel."

He let go, head tossed back, muscles flexing as his release surged forward, pulsing his shaft inside Gabriel's mouth. The man managed a few more passes before Kei exploded, every spurt draining more of his strength until his fingers fell free of Gabe's hair, his breath rasping loud in the relative stillness. Gabe hummed, the tiny vibrations drawing a moan from deep in Kei's chest. Christ, the man was trying to kill him.

Gabe chuckled as he released him, dropping a kiss on his hip. "Not exactly my game plan. Not when there's still so much I want to do to you." He sat back on his heels. "Hands and knees."

Kei levered upright, palming Gabe's head as he pulled the man in for a brutal kiss. His mouth possessed the other man's, his tongue demanding acquiescence.

Gabe resisted, tsking once he'd pulled back. "Not submissive. In fact, I quite like having you at my mercy."

"Don't think it'll be like this every time. I like to be in charge just as much."

"Then I guess we'll have to take turns. Which means it's still mine. Hands. And. Knees. I want to see your muscles move as I claim what's mine. And you are mine, Kei. Make no mistake." He leaned in close, brushing his mouth over Kei's. "You really did get more than you bargained for."

"I'm not the only one. Now either take me, or lay back while I take you."

Gabe smiled, motioning to the space in front of him. Kei nipped his lip, licking the slight hurt before flipping over—wedging himself between Gabe's thighs.

Gabe slapped Kei's ass, smoothing his fingers along Kei's spine. "I love how strong you are. How your body flexes whenever you move. You're beautiful."

Kei snorted. "You're the pretty boy in this relationship, buddy. I'm merely the brawn."

"Interesting. Then let's put that theory to the test. See how hard you like it."

Kei glanced at Gabe over his shoulder. Damn, he hadn't thought the angel would be this dominant. Not that it should surprise him. The man had said more than once that Michael wasn't the only warrior. Seemed only fitting that Gabe treated sex like any other mission—with absolute conviction.

Gabe palmed Kei's buttocks, drawing circles along his skin with his thumbs as he eased him open, pressing his cock against Kei's ass. More slick fluid soothed the tight feeling as Gabe pushed forward, slowly sinking inside.

"Christ." Kei let his head fall forward, the incessant pinching feeling stealing his breath. It'd been far too long since he'd taken a lover—and rarely had he submitted. But there was just something about having the angelic man consume him that burned deep.

Gabe stopped as his balls slapped Kei's, bending low over his back. "You feel so good. Are you okay?"

Kei hissed out a breath, moaning in reply.

Gabe ran one hand up his back, tracing the line of muscles before fisting his hair as he yanked back his head. The man's lips caressed Kei's neck. "Answer me. Are you okay?"

"Fuck, Gabe, yes, just...move. Please."

Gabriel bit at the corded flesh, humming as Kei jerked in his arms. "My pleasure."

He didn't release his hold, keeping Kei arched, their bodies touching as he slowly withdrew, pausing at the threshold before slamming back in, the force drawing another moan.

Gabe licked at his neck this time. "So tight. So fucking hot." Out then in again. "Not going to be able to stop." Another pass. "Going to keep claiming you until you give me what I want." He shimmied the bed forward this time, smacking it against the wall. "Want you shout my name until the glass rattles. No one can hear us. The entire cabin's warded. I feel the spell you tossed up last night. So don't deny me, Kei."

Gabe lowered his mouth to Kei's shoulder, sealing around his skin as he let himself go, pounding into Kei as if he'd never feel the man join with him again. Kei pushed into him, demanding more then cursing under his breath when he got it. Fire swirled along his flesh, the flames skipping over Gabriel. The man merely hummed, drawing the power into him until both their bodies gleamed a brilliant orange. Kei's chest heaved as his release burned a path down his spine, coiling until he thought his damn cock would explode.

"You're going to explode, just not like that." Gabe shifted his hand from Kei's hip to his chest. "Come for me."

He grabbed Kei's cock, fisting it in perfect sync with each stroke. The added pressure shattered Kei's control, and he let his head fall forward as he gave into the surge of pleasure coursing through him.

"Yes. Gabriel, now!"

His body convulsed as he climaxed, his seed splashing hotly against his stomach. Gabe shouted his name in his ear, stiffening behind him as he emptied inside Kei's ass, his body jerking against Kei's.

Kei's vision dimmed at the edges, tiny black dots closing in on him. Gabe's hold in his hair softened, but he didn't release his grasp as he kept Kei's head braced against his shoulder. The man's breath panted across his skin, cooling his heated flesh.

Kei glanced at Gabe, smiling at the satisfied look on

the man's face. "Christ. I've never come that hard. Who knew you had such a wicked side?"

Gabe rested his head on Kei, beads of sweat dotting his forehead. "I see the appeal of being human. I've never..."

His voice drifted off as he seemed to gaze into the distance.

Kei twisted enough to balance on one hand as he palmed Gabe's head, touching the man's lips to his. "Trust me. You're not anywhere near human, yet. But getting a glimpse at this side...can't be a bad thing. Especially, since I'd rather not let you go."

Gabe closed the last bit of distance, taking Kei's mouth in a soft kiss that bound him even more to the angel. "Archangels don't falter on their convictions. And you're mine." He smiled, gently easing free before closing his eyes as a white glow burned up through his skin. A cool, wet feeling caressed Kei's body, leaving him slightly aroused despite the numbing sensation in his limbs.

Gabriel tsked. "All I did was clean you and I can tell you're primed."

Kei laughed. "All your fault, buddy. You're just too damn tempting. And then there's those wings..."

Gabriel shook his head, shuffling to the edge of the bed before gaining his feet. He reached for his pants, tugging them on then tossing Kei his. He crossed his arms over his chest at Kei's huff. "I'm not saying I don't want you to claim me just as hard as I did you, but...we need to talk. It's time you told me how you came to be in that cemetery and exactly why Abaddon wants you dead. Other than that he seems to want the entire human race dead. But being a mage...I'd suspect you'd be useful to him. And Abaddon's far from stupid."

"That's the problem. I was useful to him." Kei sat on the edge of the mattress as he scrubbed his hand down his face. "I told you. We have a past. And it's not pretty."

Gabe's hand cupped his jaw, lifting his chin until he gazed into those brilliant blue eyes. "Nothing you tell me will alter my perception of you. It's soul deep. So stop letting those voices in your head control you and only listen to mine."

Kei blew out a harsh breath then nodded. "Fine, but don't say I didn't warn you."

CHAPTER EIGHT

Gabriel stared down at Kei, noting the warring emotions crossing his face. While Gabriel knew the man wouldn't hold back, he sensed Kei's apprehension. His doubt that despite Gabriel's promise, he'd forsake the mage once he'd revealed the truth.

Gabriel lowered onto the mattress beside Kei, smiling when the man's pants just materialized on him. He nudged Kei's knee. "Kei…"

"I know. You can feel my doubts the same way I can feel your conviction. But knowing that doesn't make this any easier."

"Think of it as a story, instead of a memory."

Kei snorted. "Right." He smiled. "You certainly have a way about you. Damn, you've got me tied in knots. Fine…"

Kei took a deep breath then pushed to his feet. He paced across the room, his hands speared through his hair, his mouth pinched into a tight line. He made several passes of the room before finally stopping and leaning his back against the wall opposite the bed. Green eyes held Gabriel captive as Kei released a sigh, shoulders slumping in seeming defeat.

"Up until a year ago, I'd spent most of my time traveling around the faery realm. Unlike this...chaotic world, I find the fae soothing. Not that they don't bicker amongst themselves. They do. Hell, those creatures can hold grudges unlike anyone else I've ever seen. But they're...civilized I suppose. And no one gave me a second look, even if my skin was on fire."

He paused for a moment, glancing toward the window then back. "It wasn't a glamorous life, but it suited me. Until I stumbled upon a demon raiding party one night trying to make my way home after sharing some mead with a friend. Granted, I wasn't quite thinking straight, but...even if I'd been sober, it probably would have gone down the same. There were over a dozen of them. And they didn't seem interested in merely letting me pass."

Gabriel nodded. "You stood your ground."

"I've always been a bit on the cocky side. Tend to talk when I should run. This was no exception." He shook his head. "I managed to dispose of about six before they really got ahold of me. Things go pretty blurry after that. Pain. Shouting. A bright light. But what I do remember is coming back to my senses face down in the dirt—men screaming nearby. I was able to open my eyes just as someone's hand grabbed my shirt. Yanked me up. Our gazes clashed. Those eyes." He motioned to Gabriel. "Is it a prerequisite that all angels are beautiful?"

Gabriel shrugged. "I prefer to believe that beauty comes from within. Makes your appearance match your soul."

"Then Abaddon throws up one hell of a glamour because his soul is fucking black—if he even has one. But him..." Kei huffed. "He mumbled something about me being reckless then dragged my ass out of there. I don't know what he did, but every last demon was dead. I remember staring at one as I stumbled past, pretty damn certain I was hallucinating."

"Why would you think that?"

"Because the creature's eyes were burned out—"

"He drained their energy!" Gabriel surged to his feet, crossing over to Kei. "Do you have any idea what that would do to him?"

Kei merely patted him on the shoulder. "I was barely conscious. None of it made sense until much later. Until it was too late, and I was balls deep in his fucking plan."

Gabriel nodded. "I assume he took you someplace safe?"

"Some cottage in a glen—not much different than this place. I passed out the moment I crossed the threshold."

"Chances are, he wanted it that way. Probably drained you of your power without you realizing it, so it'd appear you merely fainted." He gritted his teeth. "It's a miracle he allowed you to live."

"It's like you said. I was useful." Kei scrubbed a hand down his face. "I woke up the next morning. Completely healed—"

"He fell. I was there when he was cast out for atrocities so dark..." He took a breath. "I still don't know how he survived, but he'd lost his grace. He couldn't have healed you."

"Well, someone did, buddy, because it wasn't me. And at the time... I didn't know he was a fallen angel. I sensed his power…had no reason to question his claims, not when he'd just saved my sorry ass."

Gabriel raised his hands palms up. "I wasn't questioning your integrity. You're right. Unless you know the true strength of an angel's power, there's no way you'd be able to tell the difference between the small amount that remains and pure grace. Please, continue."

Kei pushed off the wall, making a few more rounds of the room. "He told me his name and that he'd healed me as a show of good faith. Faith! Fuck, and I believed him. Said he'd been sent on a mission to eradicate every demon he could find from the various realms. That it was a redemption task. A way to regain his presence in Heaven after questioning his brothers and sisters. Made one hell of a plea. Asked me to join him. Help him find his way home."

Kei turned to face Gabriel. "I fell for it. All of it. Maybe part of me thought I owed him, or maybe I just wanted to think I was part of some noble quest. Either way, I became his damn puppet."

Gabriel frowned. "I'm confused. How is killing demons evil unless…" He inhaled sharply. "He didn't."

Kei chuckled. "Good thing I can hear your damn thoughts. And yes. He did."

He shook his head. "Even Abaddon has lines he won't cross. Draining their energy and consuming their soul are distinctly different. If he did the latter on a regular basis… Christ, he'd go mad."

"Hate to break it to you, Gabe, but your brother was crazy long before that. And as I discovered, he needed the souls to perform blood spells on otherworldly creatures. Apparently—"

"It's the only way to separate a higher being from their soul. Their magic prevents an angel from merely taking it like they can a human's. An offering of sorts must be made." He stared at Kei. "I'm familiar with the ritual. And with his grace virtually gone, he'd need more than usual. That much evil... Didn't you wonder what he was doing?"

"I never saw him do it. Other than that night, when I was lucky to remember my name, he never performed the act in front of me. Always sent me off once the demons had been destroyed. I thought he was merely getting rid of the bodies to give us more time. Hide what we were doing."

Kei snorted. "Which he was, it was just for a completely different reason. He didn't want me to find them. To see what he'd done. He knew I'd figure it out."

Gabriel walked over to Kei, palming the man's shoulder. "How did you...figure it out?"

"I caught him...draining a fae. One minute she was standing there, the next..." A shudder shook through him. "There was nothing left but a hollow husk. Didn't take much to put it altogether."

"Is that when you confronted him?"

"I'd been doing his fucking dirty work for two years. You'd better believe I confronted the bastard. I considered that fae my friend—a sister. I just didn't count on him laughing. On gloating about how I'd been blind for years. Or for him to try it on me. Just my dumb luck he didn't have enough juice left, or maybe I just had more." He tapped his forehead. "Left me with a few lasting side effects, but at least, I'm still here."

"I'm sorry."

Kei shrugged off Gabriel's hand before heading for the

couch. It creaked as he sank onto the cushions, head bowed in defeat. "No one to blame but myself. I should have realized he wasn't what he claimed. Should have questioned the growing darkness I sensed, but I didn't."

Gabriel joined him at the sofa, kneeling in front of him. He placed his hands on the man's thighs and waited until Kei met his gaze. "Angels are supposed to be pure, in actions if nothing else. I can understand why your trust in him would have been absolute."

"I'm starting to dislike that word. Though, where it pertains to you..."

He smiled and Gabriel's stomach flip-flopped. The man was stunning. Kei's magic swirled to attention, covering the mage's skin in a warm red glow, drawing out a golden one from Gabriel.

Kei chuckled. "See, suppressed, not gone."

"I pray you're right. But not being able to use it has the same result as losing it. I'm weak."

"No. You just have to fight differently." That cocky grin widened. "Bet my ass you can spar with the best of them."

"It's not combat that's the problem. It's a distinct lack of power when we'll be facing beings with more than their fair share."

"Which is the part I don't get. How is it Abaddon has so much power? Shouldn't he have been drained of it when he fell?"

Gabriel tapped a finger on his mouth, some of the pieces starting to fall into place. "Unless...someone healed him, as well. Restored part of his grace."

Kei snorted. "Please, that's not something even a strong mage or fae could pull off. In fact, I'd think only God or maybe an archangel..."

Kei's breath hitched sharply as his gaze pinned Gabriel.

He nodded, absently brushing his thumbs back and forth along Kei's thighs. "It makes sense. That whoever cast me out of Heaven—healed you—has been part of this all along. Which means one of my brothers…"

Kei's hands covered his. "We don't know for sure. A strong demon—"

"Can't give an angel back their grace. Or heal one, which explains how Abaddon survived."

Kei clenched his jaw, making the muscle in his temple jump, before he nodded. "In the end, it doesn't matter how he survived. What I want to know is…why is he draining gifted and humans alike? What does consuming their souls have to do with destroying this world and more like it?"

Gabriel's power snapped in the air around them, its displeasure matching his. "It's part of an ancient soul ritual, very few creatures know exists. One that, if executed successfully, will give him the power of a dozen archangels. It'll make Michael seem but a child in comparison. But…I never thought it could be done. Few among us believe it's even real."

"I'm pretty damn sure he wouldn't go into this unless he thought he could win. Which means…it's real."

Gabriel cursed under his breath, rising to his feet before walking away. He turned once he'd reached the wall, bracing his weight against it. What he wouldn't give for even a hint of his true power.

A hand cupped his chin, raising his gaze to Kei's. "This isn't your fault."

"I've been blind to humanity for a long time. Without

direct purpose... There hasn't been a worthy message in centuries."

"Then let's change all that. Stop him before he gains his power. He's not absolute, yet." He shook his head. "I just don't understand why a righteous being would help a bastard like Abaddon? What possible motive could one of your brethren have for siding with him?"

Gabriel sighed, allowing his head to fall against the wall. "I know many see angels as pure, but... We can all be tempted. All fall prey to lies. The Abaddon I remember was charming. Charismatic. He had a way of seducing his kin into believing they were following a higher path. That he was merely helping the rest of us see our true purpose. Don't let the wings fool you. We aren't infallible, Kei. And given the right circumstances...even an archangel might be swayed toward darker intentions that have been cloaked in the light of fate."

"Which brings us back to our current dilemma. How do we face a powerful fallen angel who has an archangel guarding his back?"

Gabriel huffed. "If I had my true grace..."

Kei nodded. "Then let's get it back."

"I don't know how. What I told you is the truth. Once an angel falls..."

"But you didn't fall. Not completely. My spell snared you before you had the chance. What I feel inside you... it's far stronger than anything I ever sensed in Abaddon. That has to mean something."

"You want it to mean something." Gabriel grinned at Kei's arched brow. "But if you're right, if my power has merely been suppressed somehow...one of my brothers might be able to free it."

Kei snorted, palming the wall beside Gabriel's head as he leaned slightly closer. "Which is great, except we don't know who we can trust."

"I stand by my previous assessment. Michael would never abandon his faith."

"And if you're wrong?"

"If I'm wrong, then all hope is already lost. Even at full strength, I'm not sure I could best him. There's a reason he's God's true warrior. Why he was first."

Kei studied him for a few moments then sighed, dropping a quick kiss on his mouth. "Then our priority is to find Michael and get you healed. Any ideas on how we accomplish that?"

"Despite the fact I feel blocked, I could try calling out to him, but..."

"But then every damn angel would hear you. We might as well just ring a dinner bell over our heads because we'll have every demon hot on our asses inside of a few minutes." He furrowed his brow. "Is there any other way to contact him without the divine choir singing about it?"

Gabriel chuckled. Shit, but the man had a unique way about him. "Any call would be heard..." He paused then smiled. "But if a man of worth was to pray for Michael's help. We might be able to get a message out when Michael answers that prayer."

"And what chance is there your brother would do that?"

"If he breathes, he'll answer. He always does."

"Fair enough. Now...where do we find a man of worth?"

Gabriel motioned to the window. "There's a reason

this cabin is beside a church. The man we seek dwells within. Though convincing him to aid us…"

Kei laughed again. "Once he catches sight of those wings… Though that does pose a problem. If you don't put up a glamour, we'll be spotted the moment we step outside these walls. I can hold my own, but…"

"We only need a small measure of time. Once Michael is on our side, this war will be over before it begins."

Kei nodded. "So I give you whatever energy you need. You cloak your purity until we reach this man…then hope we make contact before we have a legion of demons standing on the edge of holy ground."

"Holy ground won't stop them, Kei."

"I know. I was just trying to psych myself up." He glanced over Gabriel's shoulder, snagging his bottom lip as he trailed his fingers along the edge of Gabriel's feathers. "Hate to see these go."

"Trust me. They'll be visible again far too soon." He palmed Kei's chest, bringing the man's focus back to his face. "You do realize, the glamour won't shield me from other angels."

"It's a chance we'll have to take. Block as many as we can. Hope for the best." He leaned in, his heart beating fiercely against Gabriel's hand. "How much of my power do you need?"

Gabriel cocked his brow, inhaling as he allowed his energy to dance along his skin. Bright, white light shimmered around them, highlighting the wispy ends of his feathers before they fluttered then faded, leaving only the ghosted hue of his power hanging in the air. "After making love twice, I've got all I need…for now."

"Good. Then this is just for the sheer pleasure of it."

Kei dipped forward, brushing his lips over Gabriel's before claiming his mouth—sweeping his tongue inside. Spicy essence filled Gabriel's senses, the familiar taste spiking his need. He smoothed his hand up Kei's chest, snaking it around Kei's head as his other fingers clenched the man's back, holding him firmly in place. Kei moaned into his mouth, the sound muffled as he deepened the kiss further, using the wall to tilt Gabriel's head slightly. Kei's magic sparked along Gabriel's skin, the soothing warmth easing some of the tension hunching his shoulders. He didn't know how the other man managed to restore his faith with nothing more than a kiss and a touch, but he knew he wouldn't let Kei down. No matter what the cost.

Kei hummed as he eased back, resting his forehead on Gabriel's. "Might be best if we both didn't sacrifice ourselves just yet. And for the record, you could never let me down. Not with those wings."

"This isn't funny."

"I know." He pressed another hard kiss on Gabriel's mouth then took a determined step back. "Okay. We head straight for the church. No side trips and no using your powers. If something comes at us, let me handle it." He held up his hand when Gabriel balked at him. "I mean it, Gabe. You need to conserve your strength, in case this gets ugly. I can handle a few demons if they pop up. Or whatever. You just focus on what you're going to say to Michael to get his ass down here. Deal?"

"Don't think I'll always acquiesce to your desires."

His smile hitched Gabriel's breath. "Wouldn't dream of it." He waved at the door. "After you."

CHAPTER NINE

Kei held his breath as Gabe headed for the door. Hell, the man still didn't have on a damn shirt. Kei muttered a few words as he released a hint of power, smiling when Gabe grunted. A long-sleeved sweater covered his torso, the blue color nearly matching the angel's eyes.

Gabriel glanced at him over his shoulder. "You could warn me next time."

"And miss having you look at me like that?"

"Like what?"

"That you're not sure if you want to punch me or kiss me."

"Both." Gabe tugged at the sleeves as if he'd never worn a shirt before. "How do you stand having all these restrictive clothes on?"

"Not everyone can prance around naked."

"I don't prance around naked. I wear armor."

"Well, today, you're wearing cotton. So make peace with it." Kei moved in beside him. "Remember. You let me handle anything that might come at us."

Gabe mumbled something under his breath, the tight press of his mouth telling Kei the other man wasn't impressed. But he gave Kei a nod then turned back to the door. The man drew an audible breath as he grabbed the doorknob, swinging the slab inward. Muted light filled the entrance, the bright cast of the sun dimmed by a heavy layer of gray clouds.

Kei walked onto the stone porch, staring across the wide expanse of wild flowers still dotting the meadow. Colored leaves twirled through the air as the breeze kicked up, bare branches swaying in the distance.

He nudged Gabriel. "Do I even want to know where we are? Besides in a cabin you call your sanctuary?"

Gabe grinned. "Surprisingly not that far." He pointed west. "Your place is down there. Who knew you'd choose a location so close to my cabin."

"Which means it won't take long for company to get here."

Gabe didn't answer, simply nodded, then headed for the church up a short rise off to the left. Who'd have thought an archangel would pick a small, mountain town as his escape? Though Kei had to admit—it felt right that he'd unwittingly settled near Gabe's sanctuary.

"So you do believe in fate. Good to know."

Kei jerked back from his thoughts, frowning at Gabe. "Who says I believe in fate?"

The man chuckled, glancing back at him. "That's what you're feeling about your decision to reside close to my sanctuary. That it was preordained."

"Or maybe we both just like the west coast."

"Rain and gray clouds by choice? You chose to be here because you were destined to be part of a higher purpose. But if you prefer to think of it as random good fortune..."

"Coincidence. That's the word you're looking for."

Gabriel just grinned, following the path as it wound toward the church. A mix of beige and gray stone rose up from the grass, a smattering of stained glass coloring the walls. Kei scanned the area. Though it seemed deserted, he knew better than to make assumptions. And knowing demons weren't their only enemies didn't sit well with him.

He sighed, watching Gabriel's hands clench and release at his sides. Though he put up a good front, Kei felt his unrest. His anguish at the knowledge that one of his brethren had betrayed him, regardless of the circumstances. Kei just hoped his instincts were right. That Gabe's grace had merely been tampered with. Suppressed in some way. If he truly had fallen...

Gabe missed a step before sighing as he stopped at the edge of the church grounds, turning to face Kei. "I can't change the past. I can only move forward. You've shown me that."

"As long as you realize you're not alone. And that I don't care whether you regain your grace or not."

A small smile lifted Gabe's mouth. "Perhaps I was the one who got the worthy vessel."

Kei stepped into Gabriel, knocking him back against the stone wall as Kei moved his mouth next to Gabe's. "You're more than worthy. I just don't want to let you down, either."

He kissed the man, allowing one brief moment of pure pleasure to course through him before pulling away. "Now, let's find this guy so we can call in the cavalry."

Gabe touched his finger to his mouth as if he could still feel Kei's lips pressed against his before heading for the front of the building. He paused at the set of steps leading up to the large double doors before drawing a deep breath. Golden light warmed his skin a moment before the doors shook then swung open, a ghosted echo of Gabe's wings flashing behind him.

"Shit." Kei grabbed Gabe. "I thought we agreed you wouldn't use your power."

"We need to see what we're up against before we step blindly into a trap."

"Ever heard of cracking a door open and just taking a peek, buddy?"

"Angels don't peek."

"They do if they don't want a horde of demons on their doorstep. And I could have opened the damn door."

Gabe glared at him. "Are you suggesting Abaddon and his minions wouldn't recognize a surge of your magic?"

Kei huffed. "Have I told you I hate it when you're cocky *and* right?" He motioned inside. "Just...try to keep the miraculous feats to a minimum."

"I'm about to remove my glamour in order to convince a priest I'm who I claim. If that doesn't broadcast our position, nothing will."

"Like I said, I hate it when you're right."

Gabe murmured something under his breath as he crossed into the church, shutting the doors behind them. Kei rolled his shoulders, trying to ease the prickly feeling creeping along his skin. He wasn't a fan of churches—or any holy ground for that matter. Not since he'd realized what he'd been party to, even if he hadn't known it at the time. It was as if his soul had been stained, and he couldn't quite shake the feeling he wasn't welcome in God's house.

"Everyone is welcome." Gabe gave him a pointed look. "And your soul is clean. Trust me. I've felt nothing but its purity since I arrived."

"Call me crazy, but it doesn't feel that way."

"The only one you need to seek forgiveness from is yourself."

Kei sighed. "Must you sound like a damn fortune cookie? And the purity is probably your soul mixing with mine. But I'll take whatever I can get. Now, let's find this priest before Abaddon finds us."

Gabriel frowned but followed Kei up the far side of the room, keeping the pews on their left. An older man with graying hair stood beside a pulpit, talking quietly to a young couple holding a baby, another child standing with them.

The small boy turned to look at them, his eyes widening as his gaze landed on Gabriel. He tugged on his mother's sleeve, but she gently motioned for him to wait, nodding at something the priest said.

The kid grinned, slowly picking his way over to them when they stopped at the bottom of the raised platform. He tilted to his head to one side, staring up at Gabriel. "Why are you hiding them?"

Gabriel arched his brow. "Hiding what?"

"Your wings." He pointed to Gabe's side. "I can barely see them."

Kei leaned in. "Up the juice, buddy. We can't have everyone knowing what you are."

"It's not my glamour. Some children can see through it when their faith is unwavering." Gabe bent down to the boy's level. "I have to hide them. So people don't know what I am."

"Are you an angel?"

Gabe nodded. "But it's a secret. Can you keep it for me?"

The kid kicked at the old wooden floor. "I guess, but... wouldn't it make people happy to see you?"

"Not everyone shares your faith."

The kid shrugged, turning when his mother called his name. He looked at Gabe one more time then skipped off, taking his mother's hand as they headed down the center aisle.

The priest walked over to them, stopping a few feet away. He seemed to measure them up, wary caution shaping his features. He straightened, looking more regal than old. "Gentlemen. I see you managed to get through the doors."

Gabriel pushed back his shoulders, instantly commanding the space. His purity seemed to pour off him in waves, and Kei wondered how anyone couldn't see him for what he truly was. "We needed make sure it was safe before entering."

A flash of uncertainty gleamed in the priest's eyes as he spared a quick look around the room. "This is a house of worship. Of God. All are safe within its walls. Now, what may I do for you gentlemen?"

"I need you to do me a favor."

The priest furrowed his brow. "And what would that be, my son?"

Gabe's jaw twitched at the man's words, but he held firm. "I need you to contact Michael. Tell him he's needed here. Now."

The man frowned. "I'm sorry. But it doesn't quite work that way. Perhaps you'd like to sit down? Find the answers you seek in prayer?"

"I can't pray, Father, or my brothers and sisters will hear me. That's why we're here. I need you to contact Michael for me. Before it's too late."

The priest pulled his mouth into a thin line, his agitation clearly showing in the lines crinkled around his eyes. "My son—"

"I'm not your son."

Kei cupped Gabe's shoulder, gently tugging him against his chest. "Easy, buddy. It's just a saying." He nodded at the older man. "Forgive us, Father. We're on a bit of a tight deadline. Perhaps there's somewhere more private we can continue this conversation? In your vestry, perhaps?"

The man took a step back. "I'm not sure who you are, but...I have nothing of value here."

Kei cringed inwardly as Gabe tensed beside him. This wasn't going at all well. He held Gabe steady as he addressed the other man. "I think we got off on the wrong foot—"

"We don't have time for this, Kei." Gabe pulled against his hold. "The sooner he knows the truth—"

"Not here. Anyone could walk through that door and see you. And the last thing we need are innocent bystanders caught in the crossfire between us and Abaddon's forces."

The priest's face drained of color as he took a few more steps backwards. "I think you two men should leave."

Gabriel arched a brow. "Do you have any idea who I am?"

The man shook his head.

"My name's Gabriel."

The priest looked at Kei as if seeking his aid.

Kei shook his head. "Gabriel. As in *the* Gabriel. One of the top seven. Ring any bells?"

The man's eyes widened, but Kei wasn't sure if it was in disbelief or reverence. He seemed to swallow with some effort before plastering on a calm facade. "Perhaps it'd be best if I got you two gentlemen some help?"

He turned just as the main doors opened, two men walking through the entrance. Their gazes swept the small church, finally focusing on Gabe and Kei.

Kei pushed in front of Gabriel. "Shit! They're demons. Gabe, get down. Protect him."

Kei bolted forward, raising a wall of fire as the demons attacked, sending anything not nailed to the floor toward him. Books and wood hissed into ashes, the dusty remains shooting into the air. Kei snarled as he countered their force, sending a stream of light toward them. It bounced off of an invisible wall, sparking into tiny arcs before winking out.

One of the men laughed. "You'll have to do better than that."

Kei gathered more of his power. "If you insist."

He muttered a banishing spell, allowing his energy to fill the room. The demon's eyes bulged wide before their anguished cries sounded above the buzz of power. Black smoke poured toward the ceiling then billowed out the door as the bodies crumpled onto the floor.

Kei sucked in a few ragged breaths, his magic flaming along his skin. He turned, frowning when the priest screamed, trying to back away from him.

The man held up his cross. "I won't be tempted by your wicked power."

Kei arched a brow. "Wicked power?" He glanced at his arms. "Oh, the fire. Sorry..." He drew his magic back beneath his skin, controlled but ready. "You've probably never met a fire mage before. The name's Kei. And you've already met my friend, Gabriel. And yes, he really is who he claims, and we're hilariously out of time."

The priest stared at them, eyes glassy, his breath wheezing through his chest.

Kei sighed. "Fuck. Just show him your wings, Gabe. We need him to contact Michael. Now."

Gabe stepped back, letting his head bow toward his chest. Kei felt his power surge then retreat, the flutter of feathers sounding through the room. He gazed at the angel, his heart swelling with pride as he took in Gabriel's majestic form. How his wings stretched out from his body, the creamy white color glowing in the sunlight. His skin gleamed as his grace swirled just beneath his flesh, leaving no doubt to his claims. The priest gasped, his hand rising to his mouth as he stared at Gabe, his breathing erratic.

Kei shook his head as he moved over to the man and grabbed his arm. "Father, I realize this is a lot for you to take in, but...we're on the clock, here. We need you to pray to Michael for us."

The man simply stood there, staring at Gabriel, his hands shaking, mumbling incoherently.

Kei snapped his fingers in front of the priest's face. "Father!"

The man jumped, finally focusing on Kei. He pointed at Gabriel. "Do you see them?"

"Yup. Guy's really an angel." He smiled at Gabe's huff. "Sorry, archangel. Now, if you'd just point in the direction of your vestry."

The man managed to move his shaking fingers off to his right. Kei nodded at Gabe, sighing as he reclaimed his glamour, his wings winking out of sight. Fuck, Kei needed to get his head on straight. He shouldn't have such a damn attraction for feathers.

Gabe chuckled. "I think it's cute."

"I'm a fire mage. Nothing about me is *cute*." He mentally flipped the man off, leading the good father behind the altar to a closed door at the end. It swung inward, revealing a large room with a desk, three chairs and a small altar. Kei half dragged the man over to a crucifix, finally releasing his arm. "Can you pray here?"

The priest nodded, glancing over at Gabriel. "What do you want me to say?"

Gabe moved in closer, his skin still a bright golden color. "Tell him you need his guidance against evil forces. That you're afraid there are demons at your door. But don't mention my name. Don't even think it."

The man frowned. "Can't you just..." He waved at the ceiling. "Pop up there and see him for yourself?"

Kei moved in beside Gabe. "It's complicated. And we don't have time to explain before another round of demons show up. So if you'd be so kind..."

The man's face got impossibly whiter. He stared at Gabriel then slowly turned toward the crucifix, bowing his head. Hushed murmurs filled the room as the man followed Gabe's instructions.

Kei nudged Gabe. "How will you know if Michael got the message?"

Gabe nodded toward the far corner of the room. "He'll come if he's able."

"So he's just going to appear?"

"Not in a way you'll be able to see him. But I'll know. Another ability we maintain regardless of our status. We can always feel the presence of another angel, even if we can't see them. Though, once he sees I'm here...I'm hoping he'll manifest in his corporeal form."

Kei nodded, not sure how to reply. They both knew the consequences if Gabe's faith in his brother had been misplaced. A grandfather clock clicked in the background as they stood there, waiting. The priest kept muttering his call, nothing but silence answering his plea.

Gabriel tensed beside him, the obvious lack of a response showing in the way Gabe's muscles clenched with every passing minute. After five, the man's breathing roughened as his arm braced across Kei's chest.

He glanced at him. "Someone's here, but..."

Kei looked at the empty space. "He's here?"

"Not Michael, it's..." He growled, his wings materializing in a blaze of light. "I know you're here, Vaasa. Show yourself before I get angry."

The air thickened, raising the hairs on Kei's arms, when a flash of energy gleamed in the room. The emptiness shimmered with a bright yellow light before a body appeared amidst a billow of smoke. Brown eyes stared back at them as the woman uncurled, rising to her feet.

A smile lifted her mouth as she glanced around the room, then nodded. "Hello, Gabriel."

CHAPTER TEN

Gabriel held Kei back, his power casting a golden glow along his skin as his sister laughed, crossing her arms on her chest. "Where's Michael?"

Vaasa sighed. "I'm sorry, but big brother is busy right now. We can't have you interrupting him."

"We?"

She tsked. "Please, don't play me for a fool. You know we rarely act on our own. There's power in numbers, Gabriel. You just happen to be on the wrong side."

"The wrong side? Since when is *good* the wrong side?"

"Don't get righteous with me. I've been fighting against the darkness almost as long as you have. I've carried out my orders like a good soldier. No questions. Nothing but blind obedience. But it's time we saw the truth." She sauntered forward, eyeing Kei. "Don't you see? We're losing the battle. Evil's winning, and your new friend here's a prime example of that."

"Trust me. Kei's as far from evil as it gets." Gabriel shook his head. "And it's not blind obedience. It's faith. I can guarantee you that whatever you've been told by Abaddon is a lie."

She arched a brow as she stopped several feet away. "Are you sure about that?"

Gabriel moved forward, ensuring she wouldn't have a direct line at Kei. "He was cast out."

"For daring to offer another option." She waved her arms out to side. "Look around, Gabriel. What he foretold is happening right before your eyes. But you're just like Michael. Like so many of the others. You've been up in Heaven for so long, you can't even see what humans have made of their paradise. How they choke the life out of everything." She shook her head. "It's time to balance out the darkness with the light."

"And how is destroying this world going to achieve that?"

"Destroy?" She sighed. "Your friend has been filling your head with lies. Abaddon doesn't want to destroy this realm. He merely wants to wash it clean of evil."

Gabriel snorted. "Is that what he told you? Told the others? How he convinced one of my *brothers* to side with him? Cast me out?"

Her face saddened. "No one wanted to hurt you, Gabriel. But we knew you'd never go against your faith, even if it is for the greater good."

"You could have asked. Explained your position." Anger burned through Gabriel's veins, sending a flash of light through the room. "What did you do to Michael? Not even Raphael would be strong enough to cast him out. Or did you convince Uriel, as well? Zarachiel? How many of you have broken your vows?"

"And you wonder why we didn't approach you. So

absolute in your convictions. Only Michael is more steadfast."

"I'm an archangel! My duty is to the light. To protect that which our Father created. It doesn't make me unyielding. It makes me strong."

"It makes you weak!" Yellow wisps curled along her skin, snapping at her apparent agitation. "Have you forgotten His greatest gift? Free will. The right to choose. To question. To do what's best even if it goes against your teachings."

Kei chuckled, giving Vaasa a bemused smile when she glared at him. "Sister, I'm not sure who I feel sorrier for— you or Abaddon, because damn, he sure has you brainwashed. And I bet he gets real sick of hearing you ramble on about the greater good when all he wants is to own you. All of you."

She hitched out her hip. "He told us all about you, Kei. About how you tried to twist his good deeds to suit your purpose. How you tried to steal his soul—gain infinite power."

Kei grinned. "Right plan, wrong guy. You've got our places reversed."

"Is that so?" She moved closer to him. "Then it wasn't you who inscribed an ancient sigil on the ground? Who cast a spell for a blood demon?"

"In an effort to stop Abaddon before he destroys all of humanity. I needed a way to get close to him, nothing more, nothing less."

"Save your lies, Mage. I saw the markings. You wanted a soulless beast to wage war." She glanced at Gabriel. "Only you would find a way to survive the fall. To save your grace."

Gabriel drew himself up, bracing his feet apart. "It's not too late to stop this. To stop Abaddon. Just tell me where Michael is."

"Michael's being held until he's needed."

"You won't hold him. He's too strong."

"No one is invincible. Even an archangel has weaknesses. Weapons and spells that can be used against him. You just have to know which ones. Michael's predictable. That's his undoing."

Gabriel bowed his head to his chest, as he dragged in a few shaky breaths. He'd never thought he'd see another battle between his brethren. Watch his kin slay each other over foolish pride. And knowing he couldn't help…

"It doesn't have to end this way, brother." Vaasa's soothing tone jerked him back from his thoughts. She smiled. "You can join us. Be part of a new beginning—one of light and peace. Of a deserving humanity. It'll be just as Father envisioned."

"If you follow Abaddon—allow my brothers to cast out those who stand against them. Destroy Heaven's most powerful weapons—they'll be no humanity left. They'll be only darkness and despair. Please. Vaasa. Take me to Michael. Let me stop this while there's still hope."

Her smile fell. "Can't you see? This *is* our only hope. Humanity will perish if we don't step in. Help Abaddon rid this world of evil. I'm sorry, but I've seen the proof. The death. The destruction. You will, too, once you let go of your false beliefs."

Her words settled heavily in his stomach. How had he missed the signs? Been blind to the unrest among the other archangels? God, how many had turned their backs on their faith? Were willing to go to war for a promise that would never come true?

A hand landed on his shoulder, the familiar surge of Kei's magic soothing the bitter ache inside his chest. He glanced at the mage, noting the unconditional support reflected in the man's eyes.

Gabriel gave him a guarded nod then turned to Vaasa. "Then you leave me no other choice, but to stand against you."

Disgust shaped her features. "We may not have succeeded in destroying you, but without access to your grace...you're powerless. Even I can kill you, now."

Gabriel released his hold on his power, allowing it to cover him in an angelic, white glow. "You sure about that?"

"Parlor tricks won't save you."

"He doesn't need parlor tricks, bitch. He's got a partner." Kei's skin erupted with flames, the heat engulfing the room. "And I'm far from powerless."

She laughed. "Do you really think you're stronger than me? I'm an angel, Sorcerer."

"And I have an *archangel* guarding my back. You sure he's truly out of juice? Got a few dead demons that will testify otherwise...if they could, that is."

Vaasa glanced at Gabriel, doubt clouding her eyes. "His grace is trapped. Held hostage like his brother. Neither can help him or you."

She raised her arms, her energy crackling in the air around them. Kei stepped in front of him, muttering a spell as his fire blazed into a wall of pure crimson. The flames hissed as Vaasa directed her force toward them, turning Kei's barrier a deep purple before shattering it and launching him across the room. He hit hard, falling to one knee before shaking off the blow. Steel determination gleamed in his eyes as he raised his gaze, his magic licking at his skin again.

"Enough." Gabriel moved between them, ignoring Kei's shouted warning. "I might not have my full power, but I've got more than enough to destroy the likes of you. I suggest you run while you still can. But know this...the next time we meet, I won't show you any mercy."

She glared at him, her energy still snapping around her. "There won't be a next time. That's why I came. To finish what was started."

Gabriel readied his stance, smiling as Kei's magic swirled around him, joining his. While he hated knowing he needed the boost, he couldn't help but drink in the power. Have it merge with his soul as the man had done. The glow on his flesh increased as any doubts or weakness faded into the background.

Vaasa's eyes widened. "It can't be. I know it's still buried."

Gabriel took a single step forward, wings stretching to either side. "I'm sorry, sister."

He focused his energy when an ear-piercing trill sounded through the room. Vaasa screamed, looking upwards before her light seemed to explode in every direction, leaving nothing but a ghostly shadow on the wall. The room shook, pictures and crosses clattering to the floor before another burst of light filled the space, finally dimming into a weak haze. A man knelt in the space Vaasa had occupied, his head bent, his tattered wings hanging at his sides. He groaned then looked up, tired, brown eyes staring at Gabriel.

Gabriel inhaled sharply, holding Kei back when the man stumbled up beside him. "Raphael?"

Raphael staggered to his feet, bracing his hand against the wall when he swayed sharply to his right. He waved off Gabriel's step toward him, doing his best to draw himself up. Blood marred his white tunic, with slashes covering both his arms. "I need you to listen. There isn't much time."

Gabriel knocked Raphael's hand aside as he reined in his power, shouldering the man's weight and helping him over to one of the chairs. He cursed inwardly when the archangel collapsed onto the hard surface, his blood dripping onto the floor. "What happened? Who did this?"

Raphael shook his head. "Uriel. Orifiel. More than I could count. It's complete chaos. Battles being waged in every realm. They..." His words slurred into a groan as his head fell forward.

Kei knelt in front of the man. "Do you know where they took Michael? If we could get to him...have him heal Gabriel's grace—"

"It's too late. He's... You'll never reach him alive. I tried and failed." Raphael glanced at Gabriel. "If I had the strength to try to repair what they've done to you, brother, I would. But that was the last of my power." His shoulders slumped. "So few of us left. Zarachiel...I couldn't save him."

Pain ricocheted through Gabriel's chest, the sheer weight of it making it hard to breathe. How had it come to this? How many of his brethren had he lost without raising a finger to help?

Kei clasped one hand over his as he stood, glancing around. "Not your fault. There's a reason they got rid of you and Michael first. But none of that matters. We can't stay. Everyone knows we're here, by now." He nudged Raphael. "Come with us. Until you regain your strength. I'll do all I can to keep you and Gabe safe."

Raphael shook his head, staggering to his feet. "Despite my weakness…they'll sense my grace. I'll only get you killed." He turned to Gabriel. "You're the only one who can stop this. They'll have a harder time tracking you with your grace buried. You might be able to surprise them. I'll keep them occupied. Distracted. But it takes all I have just to stay a few moments ahead of them. They've got weapons that cut through us as if we were mortal. You have to stop Abaddon before he consumes enough souls…" He coughed, bits of blood splattering across the floor. "I've tried pleading with them. But they won't believe me. No one thinks the soul ritual is real. That it can be done. And we've all witnessed the increase in evil. Wars. Famine. Acts of terrorism. There's little on this earth to dispel his claims. We waited too long, brother. Left them alone, too long."

Gabriel shook his head. "It wasn't our decision to make. They must choose the light. We've always known that. Do you know how close Abaddon is to completing the ritual?"

Raphael shook his head. "Only rumors. But he must be close to have risked casting you out. Trapping Michael. That set everything in motion. Trust no one but the mage." The archangel nodded at Kei. "You've proven yourself more than worthy. I'm counting on you to have Gabriel's back."

Kei glanced at Gabriel. "I'll die before that bastard lays a hand on him."

Raphael smiled. "Who'd have thought the fate of the world would come down to a fire mage and a broken angel? Godspeed."

The man closed his eyes, the air sparking around them before he vanished, leaving a strange void in the room. Gabriel braced his weight on the back of the chair, a thousand questions tumbling through his head, least of all how the hell they were supposed to stop this when he didn't even have access to his grace.

Kei cupped his shoulder. "Look at it this way. It's still there—like I've been saying all along. Which means we can get it back. But we'll have to work that out later. We need to leave. Now." Kei grabbed his hand, leading him toward the door.

Gabriel glanced at the priest as they passed by. "Thank you, and...sorry for the mess. If we live through this, I'll come back—"

"No!" The man held up his hands, shaking his head as he stared at the ghostly shadow stamped on the wall. "It's fine. You don't have to come back."

Kei chuckled. "And just like that... Let's go, Gabe. We can restore his faith later—if we're still alive." He pointed to another door on the far side of the room. "Father? Where does that go?"

"My personal quarters."

"Perfect. Gabe, this way."

Gabriel muttered under his breath. Why was it humans always sought proof, connection, then balked when they got it?

Kei chuckled again. "It's not seeing you that scared the shit out of him. It's the angelic battle you three waged in his vestry. Gotta admit...even I was a bit in awe. Remind me not to get on your bad side once we get your grace back to full strength. I'd rather not become a smudge on someone's wall."

Gabriel frowned, following him through the door toward another at the rear of the room. "I'd never hurt you."

Kei sighed. "It was a joke. I'm trying to lighten the fact we've probably got fifty damn demons waiting outside for us. Some angels, too, I bet."

Gabriel reined in his power. Now wasn't the time to waste it, especially when he knew Kei was right. They'd more than broadcast their location. Gabriel just hoped demons were all they faced. Despite his claim, he wasn't sure he'd be able to kill his own kind. Not unless they struck first...or attacked Kei... He fisted his hands at the thought. Cold fucking day in Hell before he allowed the other man to suffer because of him.

"Easy, Gabe. We're still alive. Let's just see how far..."

His words morphed into a curse as the far door sprang open, a man and a woman crossing over the threshold. They turned toward them, black eyes gleaming in the light. Kei didn't falter as his power surged forward, two streams of fire shooting out from his hands, obliterating the demons before they'd taken a step. The door snapped closed, then opened again, a dozen more gathered beyond the threshold.

Kei switched directions, sending another blast at the demons before crossing back into the vestry. He yelled at the priest to take cover as he muttered more words. Gabe suspected he'd magically sealed the room, but even Gabe knew it wouldn't hold for long.

Kei marched across the front of the altar, his pace

steady, commanding—the certainty in it comforting. "We'll try the front. If it's just as bad, we'll head for the stairs…see if we can get to the roof somehow. Blast a line through them from up there."

"I can take out enough to give you a chance to run—"

"And leave you? No fucking way. I meant what I said to Raphael. Not going to let anyone get to you while I'm still breathing. And you know that has nothing to do with saving the fucking world. Now keep your ass glued to mine."

Gabriel's power prickled his skin. It didn't like being rescued. Coddled. He was an archangel. The Hand of God. Hiding behind others twisted his gut. Gnawed at his soul until simply breathing was a feat. It shouldn't be this way. He was stronger than this.

Kei squeezed his hand. "I know how fucking powerful you are. But until we learn how to tap into it—getting yourself killed over your pride isn't helping."

"You're not much better. I sense how drained you feel."

"Like I said before. No use saving some if we're dead. And you've already proven you can carry me, so…"

Kei winked at him. Actually winked, despite the worry creasing his brow. He dashed down the aisle, nearly reaching the end of the pews before the doors swung open. He stopped, glancing off to his right as more demons stepped out of the shadows, effectively trapping them within a misshapen circle.

Kei mumbled a curse, pushing Gabriel backwards toward the pulpit. "I'll make a path. You get your ass through it."

"Not without you."

He glanced at the man, flames already licking along his arms and shoulders, encasing him in a fiery red glow. "You heard Raphael. It's up to you. I promise I'll follow, but..."

He didn't finish, his expression clearly conveying the rest. He scanned the room, drawing more of his magic to the surface. It radiated off him, spilling over and skittering along Gabriel's flesh—calling his power forward. Kei muttered something about Gabriel saving his strength as he sent a wave of fire out at the demons. A few fell to their knees, but most seemed to block it, curling the flames upwards. Snarls filled the room, the combined force of their power closing in around them.

One of them stepped forward, grinning at Kei. "So predictable. Fire. Spells. We know how you fight. And we're prepared."

Kei smiled back. "Fire isn't my only weapon."

He spun, channeling a bolt of light at the pulpit. The papers blazed to life, quickly turning to ash as the air hissed in response. He waved his hands, swirling the red glow across the ceiling, spinning it above them.

The demon laughed. "Charred paper? Hoping those Holy Scriptures will rain down upon us and smite us?"

Kei shrugged. "You've got the rain part right."

He closed his hands into fists, drawing back the magic. Gabriel felt it hit the other man, restoring a bit of his strength as the air thickened into a cloud then dissipated, falling all around them as a heavy mist.

The demons screamed as their skin bubbled, taking most to their knees as wisps of smoke curled up from their flesh, every drop igniting a new patch.

Kei grabbed his hand again. "Stairwell. Now, before the effects of the holy water wears off."

Gabriel followed behind him, mind spinning. "You condensed the vat of holy water then rained it over them?"

"Don't sound so surprised. I know a trick or two. Which reminds me. We need salt. Iron. Anything we can use against them. I had those supplies at my place, but I couldn't help but notice there wasn't anything at yours,"

"I've never needed anything, but my grace."

"Times have changed. We'll have to make do until we can arm ourselves better."

Kei blasted their way through the writhing demons, heading for the far side of the room and what appeared to be another door set into a small recess. Candles flickered to life as his magic engulfed the area, chasing away the shadows.

Kei motioned to the door. "Open it. I'll try another banishing spell, though not sure it'll work on this many."

Gabriel muttered under his breath as Kei magically cut a line across his palm. The mage couldn't afford to give up more of his blood. Or power. Anger burned hot in Gabriel's veins as he twisted the handle and yanked open the door, blinking as sunlight glared through the opening.

Kei glanced back. "Great! It leads outside. Now run, I'll catch up."

"We go together or not at all, Kei. I'm not leaving you here."

"Just start moving while I cast this spell, I promise... Fuck! Get down!"

Kei launched at Gabriel, catching him around the torso and reeling him backwards just as a stream of light shot through the doorway. The force tossed them across the floor, landing them in the center of the chamber. Pain pulsed through Gabriel's body, dimming his vision at the edges with tiny black dots. A groan sounded beside him—an echoed stab of pain clenching his chest.

He rolled, inhaling as he stared at Kei, the man's shoulder blackened and bloody. A curl of smoke rose from the wound, the scent of burning flesh filling the air.

Gabriel scrambled onto his hands and knees, cradling Kei in his arms. The man's ragged breaths skirted across his torso, his face twisted into a grimace. Footsteps scuffed around him, a chorus of laughter drowning it out. Gabriel glanced over his shoulder, watching as the circle of demons stumbled to their feet.

The one who'd talked to Kei grinned, wiping bits of charred flesh off his face. "Looks like you're out of luck, angel. Your only line of defense is down for the count. I can't wait to see what Abaddon does to the mage. I bet it'll be slow and painful."

Gabriel calmed his mind, feeling Kei's power course through him. His answered, breaking free of whatever barrier had been holding it captive. His wings unfurled, the feathers gleaming pure white as his grace awakened, filling him with blinding light. He tipped back his head, unable to control the surge of energy that gathered beneath his skin then expanded outwards into every crevice—extinguishing every shadow. Screams echoed in the background as an image formed in Gabriel's head a moment before the world shifted, and darkness descended.

CHAPTER ELEVEN

"Kei!"

Kei groaned, rolling his head to the side, wincing at the steady strum of pain in his head.

"Kei. Damn it, man, you've got to wake up."

Kei blinked open his eyes, groaning when someone shook him, igniting a new pain in his chest and shoulder. He waited as the images finally blurred into substance, a dimly lit room materializing out of the darkness. A face loomed over him, the familiar tilt of the man's lips making Kei sigh.

"Greyson?" His throat protested the single word, the dry sensation making him cough.

"Here, try to drink some water."

Greyson snugged an arm under his torso, lifting him enough to place a cup at his mouth—dribble some water across his lips. He swallowed a few sips, holding back a grunt as more pain thrummed through his body. Christ, he hurt.

Greyson tsked. "Of course you hurt, you stupid son of

a bitch. You had a gaping wound across your chest and shoulder. Looked like you'd been struck with lightning. I healed you as best I could, but..." He sighed. "We both know healing was never my forte."

Sadness touched the man's words, a stark reminder of all he'd lost. The sister Kei hadn't been able to save from Abaddon.

Kei attempted a small, half-smile. "Thinking you probably still saved my life, you bastard. Now, I owe you."

Greyson chuckled. "You already owed me. Hasn't made you visit, recently."

Kei released a painful breath. "I would have come if I could have. That's the purpose of being banished. You can't return..."

His voice trailed into a rasp. He was there. In the faery realm. But...

He pushed himself upright, trying to ignore the way the room swam as his vision dimmed. "What? How?" Memories shuffled inside his head, a single image replaying through his mind. "Gabriel!"

Greyson placed an arm across Kei's chest. "Easy. Your friend's okay, just...out. Been that way since you two materialized inside my damn home. One minute, I'm cooking dinner, the next there's a flash of light, and you're both crouched in the center of the room. He just looked at me, then keeled over."

Greyson pointed at the far wall. Gabriel was sprawled across a lounge, arms and legs dangling off the edge. His wings covered half his body, the edges brushing the stone floor.

Greyson smiled. "I've never met a real angel before.

Well, not one that hadn't already fallen. Honestly, I wasn't even sure any still existed."

Kei snorted. "You're a damn faery. Of course you knew they existed."

"Hey. They haven't been seen in centuries. That's a long time, even for my species. And whether you want to acknowledge it or not, even angels can die, Kei."

The words hit home, and he slumped back, allowing Greyson to shoulder his weight. "How long have we been here?"

"A few hours. Been trying to rouse you since I fixed that crater on your shoulder." He arched a brow. "Want to tell me what happened? Why you're paired up with an angel? After everything that happened with Abbadon…"

"Gabriel is nothing like that evil prick."

Greyson held up on hand. "Whoa. Stand down. Wasn't implying he was. I'm just surprised you trusted one, is all."

Kei let his head fall back against Greyson's shoulder. "What a fucked up mess. Help me up. I need to check on Gabe. Then we can talk."

Greyson levered him up, keeping one arm around his waist as he guided Kei across the room. "Hold on a moment. Gabriel? His name's Gabriel? As in one of the seven…"

Kei smiled. "I know. Blew me away, too. Call me crazy, but archangels shouldn't look like that. Or get under your skin so damn easily."

Greyson stepped back, his hand going to his mouth before he shook his head. "You're involved with a fucking archangel? And not just any—we're talking second to Michael? Christ, Kei. And I thought you had a death wish before. But this…" He snorted. "You're insane. You know this will only make Abaddon want to kill you more, right?" He raked a hand through his hair. "So…what's the story? Shouldn't your almighty friend here be walking around, smiting everything and everyone?"

"It's…complicated. His grace is…trapped. Though I can't help but wonder how the hell he transported us here. Last thing I knew, I got hit, and we were in a church, surrounded by demons."

"How do you trap an archangel's grace?" Greyson waved at Kei's glare. "Sorry. Obviously, if you knew that, you'd have fixed it by now. How'd you two connect?"

Kei sat down on the edge of the lounge, brushing Gabe's hair back from his face. God, the man was stunning. And knowing he'd risked his life to save him… "I summoned him. By accident, of course."

Greyson whistled. "You summoned an angel? An archangel, by accident?"

Kei frowned, grazing his fingers along Gabe's cheek, noting the pale cast to his skin. Damn, he must have given up more than a bit of his power. He nodded. "Yes. Why?"

"Call me crazy, but… Something tells me it might not have been an accident. What kind of spell did you use?"

"Blood. With a fire enchantment. I was trying to get a blood demon."

"And you got an archangel?"

"Is there something wrong with your hearing, Greyson? Yes. I tried to summon a blood demon and got Gabriel—the fucking messenger of God."

Greyson chuckled. "Well, I'll be damned. You've fallen for him. And not just a bit. You're in love with him."

Kei let his head bow to his chest. Now wasn't the time

for Greyson to go off on some tangent. "Focus, Grey. My feelings aren't the issue."

"Does he love you back?"

"Grey!"

"Fine." The man shuffled over, grabbing a chair before scraping it across the floor. "You said his grace has been... trapped. How so?"

"I don't know. But he's weak. I can sense his power..." he tapped his chest, "...in here. Like a damn heartbeat, but... He can't wield it. Can barely muster enough juice to put up a glamour. I've been recharging him—"

"I bet you have."

Kei ignored the remark. "It's minimal."

"Yet, you're sitting in my home, in a realm you were banished from."

Kei huffed. "I know. Nothing makes sense."

Greyson pursed his lips. "Was this the first time Gabriel was able to harness his power since you summoned him?"

"Not really. I've given him some of mine in order to fuel his glamour. And he saved me once before. Transported us to his sanctuary when we were cornered at my place, and I couldn't even stand up."

"So...when your life if in peril, or you're weakened, his grace comes out to play."

It wasn't a question, and Kei couldn't stop from running the words over in his head. Was it that simple?

Greyson gave Kei's shoulder a pat. "That spell you used. I don't suppose you included any binding sigils?"

Kei's head snapped toward the fae. "How did you know?"

Grey shook his head. "Kei. How many times have I

told you...tokens and words have meaning. All of them."

"Feel free to stop sounding like Gabe any time now."

"Wish I could, but your archangel is right. Which means you bound the man to you, didn't you?"

"So he says."

"Christ." Grey scrubbed a hand down his face. "Though I can't be certain without seeing you perform the spell again—and no, that's not an option—I'd guess his grace is somehow woven into your magic. There, but not accessible until you give up enough of your power he can break the hold on it. Though, I suspect it's not really something he has a lot of control over. God, if you'd seen his face..." Grey sighed. "He looked as if he'd just gone supernova without even trying."

Kei stared down at Gabe, running Grey's words over in his head. As much as he hated to admit it, the fae's theory seemed to fit. "How the hell do you know all of this when Gabriel doesn't even have a clue what's wrong? When no one seems to know?"

"You know my race is extremely old. And we have a habit of keeping all of our texts. Hell, I'll bet my left wing you got that spell from one of the Elders' books."

"You're an ass."

"Probably. Besides, since when have angels ever had to rely on enchantments? Especially archangels like Gabriel? From what I understand, he snaps his damn fingers and demons or humans simply vanish." He leaned forward. "This is out of their realm, Kei. I bet even Abaddon is scratching his head, wondering where he went wrong. What did they do? Try to cast the poor man out? Hope he fell and either died or lost his grace to the point he'd be nothing more than a glorified human?"

"Now you're just scaring me."

"I may have taken a tiny peek inside your head when I couldn't wake you up." Greyson smiled. "I will say this... he's the only thing on your mind."

"If you'd already read my thoughts, why the hell did you ask all those questions?"

"Because your mind's a jumbled mess. All I got were bits and pieces. None of which made sense until now. Trust me. If I'd known he was Gabriel—*the* Gabriel—I would have called in reinforcements. Just in case."

"He's a good man, Grey. Far more worthy than I deserve."

"Fairly certain he'd say the same about you. And he's not a man. They're going to come looking for you two, aren't they?"

"Sooner than we'd like. I'm actually surprised there isn't a legion of demons and angels at your door already." He carded a hand through his hair. "It's far worse than we ever imagined. Abaddon's got some of Gabe's brothers on his side. Convinced them he's only trying to rid the world of evil. Give it back to the righteous. The deserving. By the time they all realize his true intentions...it'll be too late."

Grey's mouth pinched tight before he nodded. "Then I suppose we'll have to figure out a way to stop them. Is there anyone you trust?"

"Michael. But Raphael said it was impossible to get to him. They've trapped him somehow. Somewhere. Not sure I want to know why. We both know it can't be good." Kei huffed. "We need a damn miracle."

"Or a really good spell."

"Greyson..."

The man merely smiled, looking far too at ease with what Kei had just revealed. Kei focused on Gabriel again, fighting the urge to run his hands along the man's body— ensure himself he was okay. Tiny flecks of gold warmed Gabe's skin just below Kei's fingers, the angel's power reaching out toward Kei. Kei's responded, adding a red hue to his skin.

Greyson clapped his shoulder. "See? It's part of you, now. Just like him." He straightened. "I need to get a few supplies. I'll leave you two alone, just do me a favor and stay inside. I've warded the hut against everything." He cocked the corner of his mouth up. "And I mean, everything. You'll be safe as long as you don't venture beyond these walls. Rest. Your...friend should rouse by morning."

Kei shook his head at the amused look on Grey's face as the man grabbed a pack then headed out the door. The tune he was whistling slowly faded, leaving Kei alone with Gabe. Kei sighed, allowing himself the simple pleasure of stroking his lover's arms, smiling at the way his muscles flexed beneath his touch. Even asleep, he reacted to Kei.

Kei trailed his fingers along Gabe's wings, marveling at the velvety feel of his feathers. The man had looked every inch the warrior angel when he'd confronted Vaasa, allowing Kei to fuel his power. The way Gabe's skin had glowed a brilliant white... Kei had never felt such pure energy before. He couldn't imagine the amount it had taken to break Abaddon's spell and transport them both here. How Gabe had even known to come here. He sighed. He'd get answers once Gabriel had recovered. Until then...

He cupped Gabe's jaw, brushing his thumb along the man's cheek. "Gabriel?"

The angel groaned, grimacing in apparent pain before opening his eyes slightly. They looked dazed. Unfocused.

Kei dipped down, taking Gabe's mouth in a soft kiss. "Gabe."

Gabe gave him the barest of smiles. "Sleep with me."

The words were slurred, broken, but they hit Kei full force. He watched as the angel shuffled back, looking as if the simple action took far too much strength. Gabe's wing lifted as he raised his arm, making room for Kei in front of him.

Kei lowered himself to the lounge, carefully settling next to Gabe only to inhale when the other man wrapped his arm around Kei's chest and tugged him against him. Gabe's wing settled over top, encasing them. Kei's heart raced, the innocent contact making the room spin.

Gabe chuckled weakly. "Me, too. Sleep."

Kei glanced over his shoulder, but Gabe had already faded, the pain eased from his expression. Kei closed his eyes, the comforting warmth of Gabe's body lulling him to sleep. Noises teased his senses, memories playing in his mind when someone grabbed his shoulder, nearly shaking him off the lounge. He jolted awake, blinking back the fuzziness when Greyson leaned down, holding his finger up to his mouth as he glanced toward the doorway.

Kei cursed inwardly at the hint of fear in his friend's eyes, nodding his understanding. Greyson motioned to Gabe then straightened, moving silently over to the door. Kei rolled, cupping Gabe's arm before gently shaking it. The angel inhaled, his eyelids fluttering open—nothing but blight blue orbs staring back at Kei. He smiled, wishing he could just lie there—watching the other man watch him, when Greyson tsked behind him.

"You two can make goo-goo eyes at each other once you've stopped this damn war. Until then...we have to leave."

Kei swung his feet off the edge, palming his head when the room spun. Damn, he really needed more than a few hours to recharge. "What's happening?"

Greyson crossed his arms over his chest. "Remember that part where we agreed they'd come looking for you? One of his brothers just arrived, but I don't think he's looking for a fun get-together. He's been interrogating everyone he comes across. Won't be long before he makes his way here."

"Shit." Kei glanced at Gabe as the man pushed himself upright, swaying in the process. "You think it's Uriel?"

Gabe raked a hand through his hair, spiking it out in every direction. "Uriel. Orifiel. Not sure it matters. We're not a match for either." He looked over at Greyson, his eyes widening. Confusion creased the fine lines around his eyes as he arched a brow.

Greyson chuckled. "Name's Greyson, though Kei insists on calling me Grey—bastard that he is. And yes, I'm a faery. And yes, again, you really did materialize in my home, in the faery realm. Welcome. Was hoping to chat about that, but...we're out of time." He tossed them both a shirt. "Get dressed. Use Kei's power to mask your damn wings if you need to while I gather a few parting gifts."

Gabe opened his mouth, but Kei laid a finger across his lips.

He smiled at the angel. "The man's stubborn. Best we

just do as he says." Kei cocked his head to the side as he lowered his hand. "How much juice do you need to make those feathers disappear?"

Gabe grunted. "More than you've got." He gave Kei a small grin. "I'll manage it. Even I can tell you don't have any to spare."

Gabriel bowed his head forward, breathing deeply as his skin glowed, his wings slowly fading. Sweat beaded his brow by the time they winked out, his ragged breathing filling the room.

Greyson walked back over. "Good. Now the shirt, and we're out of here."

Kei stood, slipping his arms through the opening, wincing as the movement pulled on the wound on his chest. "I thought you said you'd warded this place against everything."

Greyson placed a hand over his heart. "Are you questioning my competence? That hurts, Kei."

Kei merely stared at him.

Greyson sighed. "Archangels don't always play by the rules. And I'm not willing to risk your lives on the power of my sigils, especially since I didn't realize what I was up against until you revealed angel-boy's true identity. Now stop jabbering and get over here. Both of you."

Kei offered Gabriel his hand, sucking in a sharp breath at the jolt of power that passed between them when Gabe's fingers threaded through his. Gabe stepped into his personal space, dropping a quick kiss before walking over to Grey, their fingers still entwined.

Greyson watched them, amusement shining in his eyes. "Guess that answers my question."

Gabe frowned. "What question?"

Kei gave Grey a light punch in the shoulder as he looked at Gabe. "Never mind. Now explain to me how we're getting out of here without Gabe's brother spotting us? Gabe's glamour doesn't work against other angels."

Greyson snorted. "Do I look like I was born yesterday? I know that. Grab my arms."

Kei shook his head as he clasped his friend's forearm. "Grey. I don't think…"

His words trailed into a gasp as the air shimmered around them, a blue glow filling the room before the surroundings shifted, streaking the light backwards. Kei's stomach dropped as the scenery jerked back into solid form, the familiar surroundings catching his breath.

"Damn it, I hate it when you do that." He glanced at Grey. "My place?"

Greyson shrugged. "Always easier to go somewhere you know. And don't take this wrong, but…angel-boy here requires a lot of energy to transport. I couldn't risk going somewhere new."

Kei grabbed Gabe as he swayed. "Fuck, Gabe. You're not strong enough to hold that glamour."

Gabe offered him a weak smile. "We can't take the chance I'll give us away."

"Oh, bloody hell." Greyson tipped back his head, muttering words as his blue light filled the room. Ancient tokens appeared on the walls and ceiling beside the remnants of Gabe's as Grey's voice trailed off, the light finally fading. He rolled his shoulders, exhaling a slow breath. "You can lose the glamour. Those tokens should keep you safe from both sides long enough to regain some of your strength. They're far stronger than the ones I'd use on my home. Might even give you time to plan your next move. Which reminds me..." He held out a pouch. "Take this."

Kei accepted the offering, opening the top and peeking inside. "A spell book and a flute?"

"There's an enchantment in there you might find useful, though it's...risky. Hell, it's damn near suicidal, actually. As for the flute...it's a summoning instrument. One drop of the player's blood and it'll call forth a single item from their possessions." He motioned to Gabe. "Thought your angel might have something from home that could come in handy, seeing as he can't really go back there right now." Greyson stepped back. "I wish I could do more, Kei, but... I can't let this war destroy my world. My kin are amassing an army as we speak. Preparing for the inevitable attacks—that's if Gabe's brother hasn't left us in ruins already. I'll do what I can to slow him down. Keep him occupied."

"You don't have to do that. He'll kill you if he finds out you helped us."

Greyson sighed. "You risked your life to try and save Sirena. Got banished for your troubles. I owe you no less." His magic swirled up around him. "Remember what I told you. You're bound. In every way."

The light blazed brighter, blinding Kei for a moment before Greyson vanished, nothing but a strum of his power left behind. Kei stared down at the pouch, wondering what kind of spell the fae had found that he thought would help, when Gabe fisted his shirt. Kei looked up, pinned by the gleam in Gabe's eyes.

The other man clenched his jaw, his wings unfurling in a flash of creamy white. "It would seem we need to talk. What did Greyson tell you, and how else are we bound?"

CHAPTER TWELVE

Gabriel stood there, hoping he didn't pass out, as he waited for the mage to reply. Though, judging by the look on Kei's face, the sorcerer was obviously deciding how much he wanted to reveal.

Gabriel tsked. "I can just search your mind, if I choose. But I'd prefer to have you tell me."

"And here I thought we'd gotten past the point of you being an ass." Kei clenched his jaw, but firmed his hold on Gabriel, keeping him upright. "And it's nothing we didn't know already. Greyson merely confirmed that we're bound to each other."

Gabriel chuckled. "How did your friend put it? I wasn't born yesterday? He meant more than that, Kei."

"Did it ever occur to you that it might be best if you didn't know everything? That there's a time and a place for secrets?"

"Secrets get you killed. And seeing as I've developed quite the attachment to you, I'd rather that didn't happen just yet."

The muscle in Kei's temple jumped. "Jackass. You make it very difficult to say no. Fine. He seems to think the reason your grace is suppressed is because it's woven through my magic. That the binding sigils did more than connect us by blood. It joined our powers."

Gabriel frowned, trying to remember the tokens he'd seen inscribed in the ground. "If that's true, how have I been able to channel it, albeit, inconsistently?"

"Grey thinks it's a response. When I share my power with you, I weaken myself. That in turn weakens the barrier. And when I'm out cold…"

Gabriel hissed. "I had access, but no control."

Kei nodded. "I assumed that's how you were able to save our asses. That bolt hit me and bam…you're an archangel again. Only, the power seems to take over." He motioned to the sofa, helping Gabriel shuffle over. "So how did we end up at Greyson's, anyway? I know, for a fact, you'd never been there. Greyson was a bit…surprised to learn your true identity."

"I don't know. One moment I was holding you in my arms, then my power surged as the image of that fae's home shot through my head. The next thing I knew, we were there."

Kei sighed, settling in beside him. "Must be like that sanctuary thing of yours. Only you got my safe haven." He smiled. "You do know you broke Abaddon's banishing spell, right? And took us to a whole other realm. Probably killed every damn demon within a mile of that church, too. Seems you're stronger than you thought."

"Power without control is as dangerous as having none. As useful, too. I can't fight Uriel or Abaddon if I can't predict how my grace will react."

"At least, we know it's in there. It's a start, Gabe. A glimmer of hope."

Gabriel nodded. He was far too tired to argue. Not to mention the fact Kei's unwavering determination was one of the traits he admired most. Gabriel had never questioned his faith, his power, until now.

Kei punched him in the shoulder. "You're not questioning it. You're learning to cope without it. How to fight with only your resolve as a weapon. Pretty gutsy if you ask me. Lesser angels would have fled...or joined Vaasa when they had the chance."

"My brothers and sisters have been led astray. Abaddon's used their beliefs against them. Raphael was right. We've left humanity alone too long. Allowed the darkness to overshadow hope. Faith. Perhaps if we'd offered them guidance..."

"Men like Abaddon will always find a way to manipulate the truth. To corrupt."

"But that's the problem. He's not a man."

Kei nudged his arm. "Weren't you the one who told me even angels weren't infallible? Forget the past, Gabe. We need to focus on how we're going to affect the future. Stop this. Vaasa said there are weapons and spells that can be used against you. Hell, Raphael confirmed that. Any idea what those might be? How we get our hands on some, because it's looking as if it's you and me against an army, buddy—one that includes at least two of your brothers. I'm all for fighting the good fight, but I know shitty odds when I see them."

"We all have swords that can kill our own kind. Sadly, this isn't the first war among angels. But beyond that... There are banishing spells, sigils that will imprison an angel. But most require an archangel's blood and holy water. The token is inscribed on the ground in blood, then encircled with a mixture of both. When set alight, the markings and fire will trap even the strongest amongst us."

"Like Michael?"

"Yes."

Kei arched a brow. "Or Uriel?"

Gabriel's breath caught as he met Kei's gaze. "Are you suggesting we trap Uriel in a binding circle?"

Kei lifted one shoulder. "Your blood, a dose of holy water, and my fire...sounds like a volatile cocktail to me. One that might be strong enough to even the field just a bit."

"It's not absolute. The fire will only burn for the equivalent of seven Earth days."

"Pretty damn sure we've got far less than that left." Kei brushed Gabriel's hair back from his face, giving him a grim look. "If you have any better ideas, I'm listening. All I know is that we're up against some pretty daunting odds. Eliminating at least one of your brothers would certainly help."

Gabriel nodded. It wasn't the plan that bothered him—it was necessity of it. That he'd have to go against his family. Those he'd have gladly died for.

Kei sighed, scraping his fingers along Gabriel's neck then behind his head, settling on his nape. "We're not going to kill him. Think of it as keeping him safe until we can expose Abaddon for the lying bastard he is. Once we reveal that...I'm sure Uriel, Orifiel...whoever else is involved, will see the true path."

"I'm afraid it might be too late, then."

"You're angels. Isn't it your very nature to forgive?"

Gabriel sighed. "Must you always have an answer?"

The mage smiled and Gabriel's chest squeezed painfully tight. He twisted, placing his hand on Kei's shoulder before slowly unbuttoning the man's shirt—exposing the still raw wound on his torso.

Kei clenched his jaw as Gabriel traced the injury, his fingertips lightly brushing Kei's skin. "Gabe…"

"You pushed me out of the way. This was meant for me…courtesy of one of my brothers, yet you…" He looked Kei in the eyes. "Why? Why risk your life for me, bound or not? There's no guarantee I can even help you. Yet, you keep stepping in front. Keep saving me."

Kei scoffed. "For an archangel, you're not the quickest guy, are you?"

Gabriel frowned. "It doesn't make sense."

"Love rarely does."

A dull ringing sounded in Gabriel's ears, the full weight of those few words slowly registering. Warmth spread through his body, making him feel slightly light-headed.

Kei smiled. "Speechless? Damn, if I'd known that was all it took to shut you up—"

Gabriel slanted his mouth over Kei's, swallowing whatever else the mage had been going to say. Of all the things he'd expected, Kei saying he loved him wasn't one. While Gabriel had no doubts about his convictions, Kei was human—mostly human. And he knew his kind weren't generally quick to commit.

Kei's tongue danced along his, daring Gabriel to tangle

them together—taste the pure essence that was Kei. Gabriel loved how it matched the mage—fiery hot and all-consuming. And Gabriel knew he'd never tire of having it fill his senses. Knowing Kei belonged to him as much as Gabriel did to the sorcerer.

Kei chuckled when Gabriel finally released him. "You absolute types like the idea of belonging, don't you?"

"Isn't that what love is?"

Kei's lips curled into a warm smile. "And just like that... You never cease to amaze me."

"You caught me off-guard. I wasn't expecting you to proclaim your love."

"I already confessed that you had my soul."

"We're bound. That was somewhat of a given. But hearing you say the words means so much more. Especially in such a short time."

Kei chuckled. "Please, mages have been known to identify their mates after only a kiss. It's both a blessing and a curse, I assure you. Pretty damn sure you had me the moment you threatened to smite me."

"You can't blame me for thinking you were a demon. Though, I can't express how thankful I am I was wrong." He cupped Kei's jaw, thumbing the man's cheek. "I never thought I'd ever feel love. Not like this. As if you've branded yourself on my soul. I only hope I'm worthy of yours."

Kei's eyes misted over, but Gabriel could tell by the way the man tensed his jaw, he'd never let the tears fall. Kei leaned in, touching his mouth to Gabriel's. "Who knew you'd be the best damn screw up I ever made. Now stop worrying about worth, and kiss me again."

Gabriel fisted Kei's shirt, holding the man in place. "I won't be able to stop at simply another kiss."

"Christ, that had better be a damn promise."

Kei took Gabriel's mouth with his, demanding entrance then claiming Gabriel as if this was their last kiss. Gabriel responded with the same intensity, knowing he'd do anything to keep Kei safe. To give them a future.

Kei rested his forehead on Gabriel's once they'd separated, the man's heated breath raking over Gabriel's cheek. "Not giving up, buddy. We'll find a way to stop this." His breath stuttered for a moment. "But once it's over, and you get your grace back..."

"You'll still be mine. Time is irrelevant, Kei. And as you've discovered, my love is absolute. So I hope you're prepared for a very long future by my side—"

Kei cut him off, this kiss desperate. Consuming. Gabriel gave himself over to the moment. To the feel of the man's fingers scraping his scalp. The steady heartbeat beneath his palm. The glide of Kei's tongue across his. Kei's magic skirted over him, warming his flesh as it drew his power to the surface. God help him, but it seemed Greyson was right. But it meant Gabriel could only fight at Kei's expense.

Kei eased back, tugging at Gabriel's shirt. "Think about the damn battle later. I need you. Need this." He nipped at Gabriel's shoulder. "And yeah, I know it's not the best time, but... There's not going to be a 'best time', and if we fail I'd like to make the most of every opportunity."

Fail. The word felt so foreign. But it settled unforgivingly in Gabriel's chest. He could fail. Allow the darkness to swallow the light. Lose everything he'd spent millennia protecting—lose Kei.

Kei chuckled. "Is it even possible for you to stop thinking?"

He closed his eyes, muttering under his breath. Red light glowed around them, the sudden feel of skin on skin making Gabriel gasp. He glanced down, nothing but skin covering them.

Gabriel arched his brow. "I was getting there."

"Not nearly quick enough. I'm an impatient fucker. And God knows, if I let you linger long enough, you'll be off on another tangent."

Gabriel smiled, grazing his fingers down Kei's ribs to circle his hip. "I promise you...you have my complete attention. But if we're going to be using our power..."

He closed his eyes, allowing Kei's magic to pull his to the surface. He focused on a single thought, smiling when Kei cursed as the room shifted. The feeling faded as Gabriel opened his eyes. He had Kei backed against the far wall, the man's body trapped between his arms.

Kei scoffed. "Look who's learning some new tricks. But I believe it's my turn to claim you."

"I didn't realize there was a schedule. Besides, I've discovered I like feeling you clench around me. Knowing I'm the reason you're unraveling."

"You're the reason regardless of who's on top. But I have to say...I like this side of you."

"Which one's that?"

"The one that wants me as much as I need you." He nipped at Gabriel's lower lip. "So if you're going to make love to me against the damn wall...get on with it, already."

"Bossy. But all those images in my head of me taking you like this—the ones that aren't mine—means I'll overlook that small flaw." He leaned in, pressing his body firmly against Kei's. The man's cock jutted hard against his hip. "Besides, I've discovered I like you this way. Hard. Desperate. All but begging me for it."

"Wasn't my magic that slammed us against the wall, buddy."

Gabriel chuckled. "Never said I didn't feel the same. That I didn't want you to the point I can't see straight. Can't think about anything other than hearing you shout my name as you come all over me." He licked at the seam of Kei's lips. "How I can't wait to fill you." He kissed along the man's jaw to his neck. "This kind of need can't be rushed."

Kei threaded his fingers through Gabriel's hair, yanking his head back. "You can savor me next time. When I can breathe. Now fucking claim me." Kei moved his other hand to Gabriel's back, grabbing hold of Gabriel's wing as he caressed his way along the edge, his thumb brushing his feathers.

Gabriel's head fell against the other man's forehead, their ragging breath mixing. "You don't fight fair."

"Hell, no. Not where you're concerned. I'll break whatever rules are necessary. Best you understand that."

Gabriel stilled. He had a distinct feeling Kei wasn't talking about sex, or not just the sex. He eased back enough to meet the mage's gaze, but Kei used his hold to take his mouth—drive out every other thought but them. Here. Now.

Kei's taste filled his senses just as the man's magic seemed to wrap around him, slowly stroking down his body until it wrapped around his cock. Pleasure exploded in his core as the mage's power pumped his shaft, giving Gabriel the remembered feel of the man's mouth.

Gabriel hissed out a breath as he pulled back. "Dangerous, Kei. You're not the only one with abilities."

"Then show me what you've got, buddy."

Gabriel held the man's stare, panting through the fiery pressure moving up and down his length as he concentrated on mimicking Kei's actions with his own power. Wisps of gold curled along his skin, swirling around them before covering Kei—drawing a guttural moan from him.

His head fell against the wall, the heat surround Gabriel's cock faltering slightly. "Fuck, Gabe. Christ, I've never felt anything that damn good. It's like you're touching me from the inside."

Kei's breath panted across Gabriel's shoulder, cooling his flesh. Gabriel smiled, watching pleasure flush Kei's skin as the man's eyes squeezed shut. His muscles contracted down his body, creating dips and planes along his chest and abdomen. Gabriel's gaze dropped to the wound. Once he'd regained full control of his grace, he'd heal the man. Properly. Remove every last blemish, every trace that Abaddon had ever dared touch what was Gabriel's. All the scars Kei had gotten trying to redeem himself for his misplaced trust.

Kei tugged on his wing. "None of that matters. You've already saved my soul. Now make love to me. You. Not your grace."

His words made Gabriel's chest impossibly tighter. He nodded, gently taking Kei's lips in his, putting all he felt but couldn't express into that one kiss. Kei surrendered control, his touch softening.

Gabriel lowered one hand, smoothing it along Kei's hip to this thigh—lifting the man's leg and wrapping it around his back. Kei's cock rubbed against his, the sudden friction hitching his breath. He focused his power on his shaft, coating it with lube before positioning it against Kei's ass. Kei arched into the firm caress, using his heel to lever himself upwards.

Gabriel growled, pressing his mouth against Kei's. "You belong to me. Never forget that."

Kei opened for Gabriel's tongue, shouting into his mouth as Gabriel thrust against Kei's ass, burying the head of his cock inside the mage's channel. Hot, tight pressure encased Gabriel's shaft, the pure pleasure snapping at his control.

Kei hissed, moving his mouth to Gabriel's ear. "I'm not fragile. I want you to lose that fucking control. Show me what it's like to belong to you. The real you. The one none of your brothers or Abaddon could ever take away. The man I'd die for."

Gabriel sighed in defeat, as he buried himself completely inside Kei's ass, pausing just long enough to suck in a quick breath before pulling out—setting up a punishing rhythm he knew would take them both over the edge. Kei banged his head against the wall, his nails biting into Gabriel's scalp as his other hand locked around the root of Gabriel's wing, anchoring them together. He tilted into every stroke, slamming their bodies together as their combined power swirled around them, exploding in tiny bursts of orange light.

Kei's mouth latched onto Gabriel's shoulder, his

muffled cries only spurring Gabriel on. He leaned in closer, wanting every inch of them to be touching. Wanting to feel Kei's skin caress his with every pass of his cock.

Kei tightened his hold. "Fuck, now, Gabe. God, please, so damn close."

Gabriel focused his power, wrapping it around the man's cock—mimicking each real stroke with one in his head. Kei stiffened beneath him, his body quivering before he shouted Gabriel's name, the thick, hot evidence of his release coating their stomachs.

Gabriel bowed his head to Kei's shoulder, pushing into the man's ass a few more times before letting go—filling him with spurt after spurt of his seed. Reveling in the combined scent of their releases as it wafted around them like a heady mist. Kei clutched at Gabriel, any semblance of cockiness gone—leaving a side of the man Gabriel hadn't witnessed. One that more than humbled him.

Kei swallowed audibly, his frantic breaths finally starting to lessen. "God help me if you ever regain all of that grace. Not sure I'll live through it."

Gabriel chuckled. "I'm not sure God would be willing to help under those circumstances, but… I have no fear you'll do so much more than merely survive."

"Jackass. It's an expression." He finally let go of Gabriel's hair as he cupped his face. "You were right. I did get far more than I ever bargained for."

"As did I." Gabriel dropped a kiss on Kei's nose. "Who would have guessed a fall from grace would be my salvation. I only wish it was over. That I didn't have to watch you put yourself at risk over and over."

"Same goes for me. Especially, when I know how far you'll go to end this. Save Michael if you can."

Gabriel sighed, slowly easing free. Kei's power washed over him, the last few wisps of magic finally winking out. Gabriel nodded his thanks as he pushed back. "Abaddon must be stopped. Whatever the cost. Now, I believe we were discussing a plan—one that didn't involve me taking you against the wall."

CHAPTER THIRTEEN

Kei stared at Gabe, and all he could think was that he didn't give a fuck about Uriel or trapping him. He just wanted to stay there, in that moment. Bodies touching. Hearts beating in sync—love the man again. But instead, he nodded, mumbling a cleansing spell as he reluctantly released his hold on Gabe. Damn, but the man was addicting.

Gabriel stepped back, his muscles flexing as he moved. Kei swept his gaze the length of the angel's body, memorizing every ridge and hollow before pausing at his cock. Despite the fact he'd just shouted his release inside Kei, Gabe's shaft was still semi-erect, a drop of arousal beading the tip. Kei groaned, wanting to lick the slippery fluid away—taste the man on his tongue. He huffed, muttering another set of words until their pants materialized on them.

Gabriel inhaled, stumbling back a bit before shaking his head. "Was there something wrong with being naked?"

"Yeah, it wasn't going to garner you any answers other than how soon you could come again. I have only so much willpower, buddy, and it seems to be nonexistent where you're concerned."

A sexy smile curled Gabe's lips. "I'm not the only one who's tempting."

Kei raked his hand through his hair, tilting his head to the side. "If you want to remain naked, then zap the clothes off of us and pop us onto the bed."

Gabriel scowled. "You know I can't do that."

"Can't you? Wasn't my magic that transported us from the couch to the wall. Seems Greyson really was on to something. But it's not just when I'm weakened. Just using my power appears to draw yours out of hiding. That could come in extremely useful."

"Shifting us twenty feet when my senses are heightened is one thing. Wielding it with any precision in battle is another. But I'll contest that it's...cautiously optimistic. In a human sort of way."

"You know, it's a damn good thing I'm in love with you because most people would have run screaming by now. Or tried to kill you."

Gabriel's expression softened as he closed the distance, palming the wall behind Kei's head as he leaned in. "Don't think I'm blind to how fortunate I am. I only hope my love is enough."

He pressed his mouth to Kei's, the soft kiss more intimate than moments before when Gabe had been balls deep inside Kei. Kei slid his hand to Gabe's cheek, holding him close, savoring every shared beat of his heart until his lungs burned. Gabriel eased back, thumbing the corner of Kei's mouth before taking a determined stride back.

He rolled his shoulders. "Do I need to mask my wings in order for you to concentrate?"

"Bastard. You don't have to rub in how crazy I am about your damn feathers. And no. I think I can restrain myself without you wasting the energy..." He paused, watching the way the pearl color turned nearly transparent for a few moments as Gabriel crossed his arms over his chest.

"Kei?"

"Shit." He blew out a ragged breath. "I'm fine. But you are a beautiful distraction. Okay, now that we've taken the edge off—"

"Not sure that's even possible where you're concerned, but carry on."

Kei flipped the man off, moving back to the couch as he retrieved the items Greyson had given them. "Grey seemed to think these would be enough to at least give us a chance. Thinking it's a place to start."

Gabriel joined him, gently taking the flute from Kei's hands. "He said a drop of blood would enable me to retrieve one of my possessions. Even if it's in Heaven."

Kei grinned. "Thinking one of those swords you mentioned could come in handy. Unless there's something else that could help us more."

"My sword is one of the few items I actually covet. It was a gift."

Kei's breath caught as he met Gabe's stare. "From..." He pointed at the ceiling.

Gabe grinned. "From God. Yes, Kei. All of my brothers were given a sword as testament to our rank and our duty to uphold our faith. I'll admit. I hadn't thought I'd ever have to use it against my brethren again."

Kei placed his hand on Gabe's arm. "We'll do our best to limit any casualties among your kin. How do you feel about slaying demons with it?"

"I think my soul can stand to shed their blood."

"Good. I say we give it a try." He frowned. "You can make yourself bleed, right? Because I'm pretty sure a regular knife isn't going to nick your flesh."

Gabe scowled, holding out his hand as he placed the tip of his wing above his palm, slicing it across his skin. A red line welled along his hand, the brightness of it souring Kei's gut.

"Fuck, Gabe. I said a drop."

"We'll need more if we plan on using a blood circle to snare Uriel. Might as well gather all we need, now."

"I hate this, but you're right." He cupped Gabe's hand, holding it over the end of the flute until his blood dripped into the hollow tube. He removed the instrument, retrieving a bowl from across the room—inwardly cursing every red drop that pooled in the bottom. Gabe held fast, filling half the bowl before nodding at Kei. He placed the bowl on a small table then curled Gabe's hand into a fist before muttering a spell. His magic swirled across Gabe's fingers, sinking beneath the surface. Gabriel opened his fist, arching a brow at Kei.

Kei smiled, running his thumb over the healed wound. "I took a chance that having your grace trapped meant I might be able to at least heal physical wounds. Or maybe it just unlocked yours long enough to seal the cut. I know it's not much but…"

Gabriel cupped his fingers over Kei's. "Thank you."

Kei snorted, giving the man a playful swat. "You could have warned me your wings are really weapons."

"I enjoy the way you touch them too much to dissuade you. And they'd never lash out at you like that."

"Good because I'm pretty sure there's no going back for me." He held up the flute. "Might as well see if it worked."

Gabe took the instrument, placing it against his lips. His cheeks expanded as he blew into the stem, a soft lilting tone trilling out the other end. The air around them thickened, tiny sparks bursting in front before a flash of light filled the room, fading into a solid, silver sword balanced across the table. Gabriel reached for it, his power gleaming gold along his skin as he grasped the hilt, lifting it to his chest. Sadness creased the edges of his mouth as he rested his forehead against the blade.

Anger, regret, guilt. Kei felt them as if the emotions were his as Gabriel breathed deep before drawing himself up. He placed the weapon at his side, holding it there as his power slowly covered it, glowing bright then winking out.

Kei cocked his head to the side. "It vanished."

Gabriel smiled, but it was obvious it had nothing to do with happiness. "The sword was forged for me alone. It's part of me. Grace or not, it's mine to wield unless I choose to give it to another."

"So it's still there I just can't see it?"

Gabriel nodded, his expression confirming that the subject was closed.

Kei shrugged. "Whatever you say, buddy. Next step... making some of this binding blood mixture. You said you needed holy water."

"For the ring of fire to hold an archangel, we'll need

equal amounts of blood and water. Which means we need to visit another church."

Kei arched his brow. "But I thought anyone could make holy water with the right intentions and the proper blessing? Can't we just get some out of the tap, mutter some words and bam…holy water?"

"Not all holy water is equal in strength. In order to bind an archangel, the water must be blessed by a priest, or higher power. Otherwise, their grace can counteract the spell."

"Great. I didn't exactly enjoy our last outing." Kei sighed. "Fine. You stay here. There's a church not too far from here. I'll go…borrow a container of holy water and come straight back."

Gabe grabbed Kei's wrist. "Once you move beyond the door, they'll be able to locate you."

"A risk one of us has to take. You just said it needed to be a certain strength. Unless this is your subtle way of telling me you can bless it." He groaned. "Which makes sense. You're far more pure than a priest."

Sadness crept into Gabe's expression. "Were I at full strength, I could bless any water and give us what we need. But with the status of my grace uncertain, we can't risk that it won't be strong enough to hold Uriel. Pure enough."

"Gabe…"

"Whether I want to acknowledge it or not, it's true."

"Fine. We'll err on the side of caution, which means a trip to a church."

Gabe cleared his throat. "There is another way."

Kei furrowed his brow. "Another way?"

"Perhaps the correct phrase is...another church. One that won't give away our current location."

Kei stared at Gabe when his words hit home. He shook his head, stepping into Gabriel's person space. "No."

"It won't take me any longer than it will you, and we won't expose where we are."

"No. You'll just be out there on your own. Did you forget you just annihilated fifty odd demons at that church? You might have blown it up for all we know. Besides, how are you going to get there?"

Gabe arched his eyebrow.

"Fuck." Kei raked a hand through his hair. "It's not that I mind you draining me, it's just... I won't be much help for a few hours. Not with the amount you'll need."

Gabriel trailed his fingers down the side of Kei's face, thumbing his chin. "I'll watch over you."

Kei clenched his jaw. "There are a million ways this could go wrong."

"We only need one for it to go right." He dipped in and kissed Kei softly on the lips. "Have faith."

"Are you going to throw that in my face every time you want to get your way? Because I can assure you that once you're back to full strength, it won't work." He huffed, grunting out his next breath. "Fine. Let's charge you up and you can go scare the poor Father good and proper. But you go to your damn sanctuary and back. I swear, Gabriel, if I think you're ditching me—"

Gabe's mouth claimed his, his tongue demanding entrance. Kei relinquished control, knowing he didn't have the strength or the desire to deny the angel anything. Not when he knew this one act would turns the tides. Restore Gabriel's faith in himself or destroy any hope of winning the war. Gabriel deepened the kiss as Kei's power flowed around them, slowly fading from Kei's grasp. He didn't resist, allowing Gabe to set the pace—to take whatever he thought he needed.

Black dots swam across the edges of Kei's vision when Gabriel finally eased back, keeping their foreheads touching. Kei felt the room dip. He blinked away the dizziness as Gabriel loomed over him. Shit, Kei didn't even remember the other man carrying him to his bed.

Gabe gave him another kiss. "I'll be back in what seems a heartbeat. Rest. I'll keep you safe."

Kei closed his eyes, drifting in a hazy blur as his power slowly increased. A steady pounding thrummed through his head as he forced his eyelids open, staring off to the side until his vision cleared. Gabriel sat in a chair next to the bed, arms crossed, his gaze focused on Kei.

The angel smiled as he leaned forward, tucking some of Kei's hair behind his ear. "I thought you'd never wake up."

"Never?" He coughed at the dry rasp of his throat. "How long have I been out?"

"About a day."

"What?" He pushed onto his elbows only to fall back down. "Damn it!" He accepted Gabe's hand, allowing the other man to lever him up. He settled against the wall, his focus never leaving Gabriel. "At least, tell me you were able to do some archangel-type shit while I was out."

"Like I said. Having access to my power and controlling it are distinctly different. Though it appears Greyson was correct. It's definitely woven through yours."

"Which means you can't use it against Abaddon..."

"Unless you're unconscious."

Kei laughed. "And just when I thought we might catch a break. Did you get the holy water?"

"More than enough. I've already prepared the mixture. All we need now is a way to lure Uriel into the trap."

"Luring your brother isn't the problem. It's the horde of demons that accompany him. We can't fight them all, especially if I'm on the verge of passing out in order for you to have any power at all."

Gabe's expression sobered. "I have my sword. I can fight without the aid of my grace."

"Not against another archangel. Or Abaddon. Even if you can't wield it the way you want, it gives you strength. Or they'll kill you with a damn snap of their fingers."

Gabriel chuckled. "It'll take a bit more to than that. And I won't risk your life to save mine."

Kei sighed. There'd be no arguing with the man. Kei would just have to find a way to give Gabriel what he needed. Kei glanced at the table, eyeing the spell book. Greyson had said there was one worthy of taking a risk. Kei only hoped his friend was right.

He held out his hand. "Help me up, and we'll see if we can devise a way to get Uriel to pay us a visit without his unholy friends tagging along."

Gabe tsked, lifting Kei off the bed and carrying him over to the couch. "What? We both know you would have fallen on your face. You need some of your power back."

Kei palmed his chest. "Soon. First, let me look through that book. See if there's anything remotely useful."

Gabriel frowned, but complied, pacing away as Kei turned to the first page. He skimmed the verses, flipping through the different spells until something caught his eye. He paused, slowly reading the lines, his chest tightening with every word. This had to be the spell Greyson had thought would help, but damn... It was more than crazy. It was borderline apocalyptic.

He studied the text, mentally reciting some of the passages. If he'd thought the blood spell had been difficult, this made that look like a simple rhyme. And if he got any of it wrong—screwed up any pronunciation— God only knew what he'd end up raising. He glanced toward Gabe, but he was staring out the window, seemingly lost in thought. Kei removed the important pages, folding them then sticking them inside his pocket. Not that he wanted to hide anything from the other man, but he knew Gabe would never support trying a spell that risky. Not when success could be as deadly as failure. Uncertainty churned in Kei's gut as he considered his options, hoping they'd figure something else out before they ran out of time.

The angel appeared at his side, arms crossed, brow arched. "Find something?"

Kei schooled his features, focusing on something else entirely. "Nothing that we can use to lure Uriel. Just some ancient spells this world probably hasn't seen in over a millennium." It wasn't a lie. The spell had nothing to do with Uriel.

Gabe frowned. "Are you sure? I was certain I sensed that something was...off."

"I'm just tired."

Gabe shook his head, kneeling in front of Kei. He cupped both sides of Kei's head, stroking his thumb along his jaw. "I've done what's required, for now. You need some of your power back."

"I'll recover."

Gabe tsked, leaning in. "Stubborn."

He slanted his mouth over Kei's—a soft, slow caress of his lips—as if they had nothing but time. Warm, pure light arced across Kei's skin, hitching his breath before sinking beneath the surface. The dizzy feeling eased, his vision clearing when Gabe pulled back, giving Kei a stunning smile.

Kei pushed into Gabe's hold. "I don't think I'll ever get over how damn beautiful you are."

"I'm sure after a millennium…"

Kei grabbed Gabriel's arm as he shifted to his feet. "A millennium? Gabriel…I'm not immortal—"

"No. But you're the mate of an archangel."

"Which means…"

Gabe laughed. "How about we save *that* conversation until we've stopped this madness, and there's more than just a heartbeat of life left."

"Not funny. And we *will* discuss what that means." Kei eased back against the sofa. "Any ideas? You looked pretty deep in thought before."

Gabe glanced around the room. "Only one."

"Let me guess…the sigils."

"If we remove specific ones, we should be able to choose what's able to crossover."

"In theory, of course."

Gabe sighed. "I can't give you a guarantee. The rules have changed. Nothing is as it should be."

"You're still pure. Still willing to wage war against the darkness. That's the only guarantee I need." He waved at the markings. "How many would we have to remove to make it a one-way door for archangels only?"

"Three."

Kei coughed. "Three? That few?"

"There's a reason we're warriors of God. Not much can refuse us or defeat us."

"I realize that but... Shit."

He drew in a few shaky breaths. Now wasn't the time to back down. To lose faith. And if it worked, they'd be a step closer to being able to face Abaddon.

Kei nodded. "I'll remove the sigils once you've drawn the binding token. Just show me which ones. Don't want to let anything else through."

Gabriel pointed to the markings, then furrowed his brow. "Are you sure you're okay?"

"We're about to meet your brother, and it's not so he can welcome me into the family." Kei gained his feet, enjoying the way Gabe placed his hands on Kei's hips without even seeming to think about it. "If this goes wrong..." He covered Gabe's fingers with his. "Knock my ass out and do whatever you have to. Like I said before. There's a reason they got rid of you and Michael. They're afraid of you. Of your power. Your faith."

"I'd rather love your ass if it's all the same." He sighed at Kei's scowl. "I'll keep that in mind. But this will work. It has to."

Gabriel dropped a quick kiss, once again looking as if he didn't quite believe Kei before stepping back. He retrieved the blood, kneeling on the floor as he began inscribing the sigil on the floor. Kei watched him work. Damn the man truly was stunning. The way his arms and back flexed, creating delineating lines along his physique. Or how his wings gleamed in the light, each feather unique to the others. Kei had never witnessed such a perfect combination of strength and grace, and he knew he could spend a lifetime—a hundred lifetimes—staring at the man and still want more. More time. More love. More everything.

Gabriel paused, glancing at him over his shoulder. The man's simple smile clenched Kei's heart. He shook his head. The damn angel had far too much control over him. All it took was a single look, and Kei was lost. Determined to do whatever necessary to keep him safe.

The pages he'd tucked in his pocket felt strangely heavy. Despite what he'd said earlier, he hated keeping secrets from Gabe. But in this case... It might be their only chance. That's if Kei could even perform the ritual. The fact Greyson had considered him worthy gave Kei some hope, but...the faery didn't always think things through. And Grey was far more talented in the art of spell work than Kei was—a fact that irritated the shit out of Kei. It was as if Greyson could glance at a verse and repeat it flawlessly.

Kei pushed away the thoughts. With any luck, this trap would work and Uriel might give them something useful. Or maybe they'd be able to sway the archangel back over to their side—prove to him that Abaddon was merely using them all as pawns in a much darker scheme. One that would annihilate the very world they thought they were protecting by doing the bastard's bidding.

The soft padding of footsteps drew Kei from his thoughts. He mustered a smile as Gabe stopped in front of him, the man's gaze still wary. He glanced at the markings over his shoulder then focused on Kei again.

"All's that left is a ring of blood fire. We can hide the actual sigil, but the ring must be visible in order to burn."

Gabe cocked his head to the side. "Are you sure you're strong enough for this?"

Kei chuckled, turning his hand palm up. Flames leaped off his skin, the flickering light casting a red hue over Gabe. "Fire I can do in my sleep. It's the getting him to stand where we need him part that might not work out so well."

Gabriel's mouth pinched tight. "Leave that to me. I'll deal with my brother. You just need to light that fire."

"We'll both deal with Uriel. Partners, remember?"

"You're a hard man to forget. But unlike me, Uriel has full control of his power, and he'll use it without mercy."

"Then let's make sure he steps inside that damn sigil before he has a chance to smite me."

Gabe sighed, patting Kei on the back as he motioned to the symbols on the ceiling. "You ready?"

Kei nodded, channeling his magic. He focused on the markings Gabe had indicated, muttering a spell as he released his energy, effectively erasing the symbols. Tiny sparks played along his skin as the last token vanished, leaving a strange void in the air. Kei looked at Gabriel, nothing the way the man's fists clenched and released at his sides.

He pushed down any doubts, as he nudged Gabe. "How long before your brother realizes..."

The windows rattled around them, the noise drowning out Kei's voice. Books and furniture shook, some tumbling to the ground as a bright light flashed across the ceiling.

Gabriel turned to Kei. "He's here."

CHAPTER FOURTEEN

Gabriel stood his ground as the room shook harder, the light slowly filling the area. Kei tensed beside him, the mage's apprehension palpable. Not that Gabriel blamed him. Facing an archangel, knowing they were outmatched, was insane. The fact Kei hadn't run still amazed Gabriel.

He calmed his mind. He knew Uriel. The man liked to talk. Boast. He wouldn't simply destroy them without gloating how his path was the righteous one. Without trying to convince Gabriel to join them now that their original plan had failed, and Kei had saved Gabriel's life—and his grace.

Betrayal soured his stomach. He'd never thought one of his brothers would actually turn on him. On Michael. That he'd be forced to fight men he would have died for. A sense of calm washed over him as the air crackled then popped, the light slowly fading.

A man knelt on the floor near the door, head bowed, one hand braced on the old wood. His wings stretched out to either side, darker than Gabriel's, with the ends shaded black. His skin gleamed a bright yellow hue, as he rolled his shoulders, finally lifting his chin. Gray eyes stared back at Gabriel, the disappointment clouding them impossible to miss.

Gabriel touched Kei's arm but didn't look at him. "Stay close. Let me handle Uriel."

Kei grunted but remained at Gabriel's side as he shuffled over, bracing his feet apart as he faced Uriel. The man's gaze swung to Kei, anger flushing his cheeks. He rose, looking more than a bit intimidating dressed in his angelic armor, his sword hanging at his side. Gabriel resisted reaching for his. The weaker he appeared to Uriel, the less aggressive the archangel would be. And they needed to buy enough time to trick Uriel into the binding circle.

Uriel focused back on Gabriel, another flash of sadness dulling his eyes. "This is...unexpected, brother."

Gabriel arched a brow. "Which part? That I'm alive, or that I haven't cowered in front of you?"

The muscle in Uriel's temple jumped. "So you know."

"That it was you and Orifiel that cast me out? Hoping I'd fall to my death? That you've imprisoned Michael?" Gabriel snorted. "What I know is that you've turned your back on your faith and have chosen to serve darkness."

"Is that what you've been told?"

"Are you saying you weren't the one behind my fall?"

Uriel glanced away. "I had no choice. You..." He sighed. "You always see everything in exact terms. Your love for humanity is second only to Michael's. I knew we'd never be able to sway you. To get you to see what humanity has become." He faced Gabriel again. "They have forsaken us, Gabriel. Forsaken our Father."

162 | KRIS NORRIS

"They haven't forsaken anything. They're just lost. Confused. It's our job to guide them. To give them a reason to hope."

"Hope? Have you not witnessed the acts of pure evil they inflict on one another every day? The lives they take in the name of pride and greed?" Uriel shook his head. "*Hope* is what's *lost* on Earth."

"If humanity has turned toward the darkness it's only because we haven't given them enough light to banish the shadows. But it's not too late. We can save them, save ourselves, if we band together. Stop Abaddon from destroying this world and every other one like it."

Uriel's mouth curved into a cocky grin. "Is that what you believe? That Abaddon is out to destroy mankind?" His gaze shifted to Kei. "Has this vile sorcerer been filling your head with lies, brother?"

Gabriel stepped in front of Kei, blocking him from Uriel. "The mage is off-limits. This is between us."

"Off-limits? Since when do you defend the wicked?"

"Kei's many things, but his soul is pure."

"Pure? He's a mage! You know better than anyone the line they tread, often stepping into the dark arts in order to gain their prize. Did he not summon you using a blood spell? One designed to conjure a demon?"

"His purpose was clear."

Uriel shook his head. "He's tainted you."

"Has he? Tell me, brother, how much blood of our brothers and sisters stains your sword? How many innocent lives have you claimed in the name of a prophet who deems himself ruler over all of us? A man who will stab you in the back the moment he gets the chance."

"You forget, Gabriel. Abaddon was our brother, too, once."

"And Michael still is, yet you imprison him, and for what? So Abaddon can kill him, himself?"

"Abaddon isn't the monster you claim him to be."

"He chose to serve the darkness, Uriel. Have you forgotten what he did? The lives he took?"

"He did what he had to do to expose humanity for what it truly is! Wicked! Evil."

"It was you. You saved Abaddon after he fell. Healed him, healed Kei so he could do Abaddon's bidding. All this time, you've been scheming with him."

"Not every order that comes from Father is just. I did what I thought was right. What would save the world Father loves so dearly."

Gabriel sighed. "Abaddon shows you only what you want to see, brother. He's lying to you. He's trying to invoke the ancient soul ritual. Consume enough that he can regain not only his grace, but that of a dozen archangels. He'll be unstoppable."

Uriel took a few steps forward. "You've been talking to Raphael."

"I don't need Raphael's guidance to see what's before me. What you're choosing to ignore."

"The ritual is just lore. I've been watching Abaddon. I've seen the demons he's destroyed. The tireless work he's been doing to combat evil." He pointed at Kei. "Your mage is the one who's corrupt. The one who's trying to wage a war against us."

Gabriel bowed his head. He knew Uriel would be unbendable, but he'd hoped... Had prayed that he was wrong. That Uriel only needed to be shown the light...

Gabriel's shoulders drooped. "So you've come to kill me."

Uriel took another few steps forward, but not enough to enter the sigil. "Hand over the mage, and you can join us."

"I already told you, Kei's off-limits."

"Why? He's just another demented soul."

"He belongs to me. And I, him."

Disgust creased the lines around Uriel's face. "You've bonded with him? Chosen him as your one?"

"I have."

The angel drew his sword, holding it at his side. "Then you are truly lost, brother."

Gabriel moved sideways, hoping Uriel would follow. "What will it take to prove to you I speak the truth? That it's Abaddon who speaks in lies?"

Uriel furrowed his brow. "Gabriel..."

"My life?"

Kei shoved him out of the way. "No way, Gabe."

Gabriel gave him a small smile then turned back to Uriel. "If I bow before you—willingly give you my soul—will you free Michael and stop this madness before your soul is lost?" He moved over, silently urging Uriel to follow. A few more steps and he'd crossover the edge.

"I'm sorry. It's too late."

Uriel channeled his energy, his skin gleaming gold, as he leapt toward them, his sword cutting downward toward Kei. The mage sent a blast of fire at the angel, knocking him back slightly. Uriel caught his balance and swung again, his blade connecting with Gabriel's as he blocked the strike.

Uriel's eyes gaped wide as he took a faltering step backwards. "It can't be. I locked that away…"

Gabriel used the distraction to launch his attack, trying to maneuver Uriel toward the sigil. The man recovered quickly, countering the blows before getting the upper hand. He caught Gabriel across the arm, leaving a splatter of blood along the floor. Gabriel pivoted, blocking a hit to the head as he landed a few kicks to Uriel's chest. The man skidded back, snarling before racing forward. Metal sparked on metal as their blades connected, each blow drawing more of Gabriel's power. He clenched his jaw, stepping into one of Uriel's advances, locking the man's arm in his. Uriel grabbed Gabriel with his other hand, tossing him across the room.

Gabriel hit hard, groaning as the world spun for a moment. Blood dripped into his eye as a loud ringing sounded in his ears. The air snapped behind him, the hiss of fire drowning out the pounding of his pulse in his head. He turned, inhaling as Kei advanced on Uriel, casting some kind of spell that tumbled the archangel onto the floor. Crimson fire lashed out of Kei's hands, encircling Uriel's weapon before whipping it sideways.

The sword crashed into a bookcase, clanking onto the floor. Uriel cursed under his breath as he stood. He glared at Kei, his skin glowing brighter before he channeled his power at the mage, lifting him to the ceiling then driving him into the floor. Kei managed another shot of fire, but the archangel blocked it, taking a determined step toward the sorcerer.

Gabriel pushed to his feet, stretching one hand toward Kei, the other at Uriel. Kei's magic swirled over Gabriel's skin, fueling his power as he released it toward his brother, shielding the next blast of energy the other man directed at Kei.

Uriel huffed in frustration, spinning toward Gabriel as he marched across the room. "Enough, Gabriel!"

Gabriel held his ground, staring the man in the eyes when flames flashed between them. Uriel stopped, staring at the floor as Kei's fire ignited the blood, quickly sparking the line until the circle was complete. The room shook, the color bleeding into blue as it seemed to feed off of Uriel, the glow on his flesh dimming.

Gabriel took a staggering step forward as he glanced at Kei. The man waved him off, pushing to his hands and knees. Gabriel didn't know how Kei had the strength to stand. He'd given up so much of his power...

Gabriel made his way over to the circle, sheathing his sword, his gaze fixed on Uriel. "You gave me no other choice."

Uriel glared at him, studying the flicking light. "Do you really think this will change anything? That it'll somehow allow you to seize control?"

"I did this partly for you. To keep you safe until it's over. Pray there's still a way for you to find your path back."

"Back to what? You're the one who's fallen."

Kei snorted, stumbling over, colliding with Gabriel before he seemed to gain his balance. "You cast him out, you son of a bitch. Didn't even give him a chance, and yet he still shows you mercy. Traps you instead of killing you."

Uriel arched a brow as he crossed his hands over his chest. "I wouldn't have lost."

Kei shook his head. "You already did. You betrayed your brothers."

Gabriel huffed. "Where's Michael?"

Uriel laughed. "It doesn't matter. Even if I told you, you'd never reach him alive. I'm not the only line of defense, and you're weak."

Kei chuckled as he dabbed at the blood on his face. "Says the man trapped inside the blood sigil."

"Which will only hold me for seven days." Uriel cocked his head to the side. "I'll still be alive. Will you?"

Fire sprang to life on Kei's arms. Gabriel ran his fingers along Kei's skin, smiling when the flames dimmed then vanished.

"Tell me, brother. What did Abaddon promise you? What price bought your soul?"

Uriel sneered at him. "And you wonder why we didn't come to you? You and your righteous beliefs. Never wavering. Never questioning. Father always did like you and Michael best. The good sons. The obedient sons."

"I follow because I have faith. Because I see the good in humanity."

"What good is faith when it's misplaced? Tell me, Gabriel, how many of your precious humans would come to your aid? Would stand beside you and face the wrath of a thousand angels? Would risk their souls against an army of demons?"

Gabriel sighed. "All I need is one. A single soul whose courage restores mine. A reason to fight." He looked at Kei. "I was lucky. I was given so much more." He inched closer. "I know you think the ritual is lore. That it can't be completed, but I swear to you—Abaddon is about to do just that. All these demons he's been hunting—his proof of goodwill—it's just a ruse. A means to extract the souls of other higher beings. Kei caught him in the act. Was banished and nearly killed for his actions. Once Abaddon consumes enough...he'll have absolute control. And he'll destroy humanity and Heaven and every other realm he can to slake his lust for power."

Some of the arrogance lifted from Uriel's expression. "How do you know your mage speaks the truth?"

"Because I feel his soul. It's bound to mine."

"Sorcerers have been known to fool—"

"He summoned me, Uriel. As his worthy vessel. Me!"

Uriel's mouth gaped open as his hands fell to his sides. "That's how you survived? So it wasn't just any blood spell, it was an ancient soul spell?"

Kei cleared his throat. "A what?" He nudged Gabriel. "You never said anything about a soul spell."

Gabriel nodded. "We were already bound. I didn't see the point, but... You couldn't have gotten me if our souls weren't already connected. If you, in turn, weren't worthy of mine."

Kei shook his head. "I don't understand."

Uriel mumbled something under his breath. "It means that you and Gabriel were fated to be. But..." He drew a deep breath. "It matters not. Just because his soul is worthy of yours doesn't prove your theory. It just means that your fall from grace was written long before I helped cast you out. That it's your worth that's in question."

Gabriel fisted his hands, doing his best to rein in his anger. "How can you be so blind?"

"It's a matter of perspective, brother. I choose to see it from another angle. One that isn't overshadowed by wishful thinking." Uriel waved his hands to the sides.

"Look around you. The proof of Abaddon's claims are everywhere."

Kei's hand landed on his shoulder. "Save your breath. He's not going to be swayed." Kei looked at Uriel. "At least we know Abaddon's going to kill his cocky ass once he completes the ritual. It's not much compensation, but I'll take it."

Uriel sighed. "You're wrong. My brother will free us. Transcend Earth into the true paradise it could have been if humanity had not lost its faith."

Gabriel huffed. "Abaddon isn't your brother. Not anymore. Michael is and you have the power to save him."

"Michael's a fool. Blind like you. But he'll be the first to see the truth revealed. That's why he's been imprisoned."

Kei snorted. "You arrogant jackass. If Abaddon hasn't killed Michael, it's because he needs him for something. There's no other reason he'd keep Heaven's greatest warrior alive. Not when Michael has the ability to destroy him before he gains his…"

Kei's voice trailed off as a pure blue light flashed through the room, billowing papers into the air. Sparks cracked overhead before the floor shook, the light glaring bright then winking out. A man stood off to their right, hair tousled, hazel eyes blinking rapidly.

Kei muttered under his breath. "Greyson. What the hell? You shouldn't be here. It's not safe."

The faery tripped his way over, grabbing Kei's shoulder for balance as he stumbled to a halt. Dried blood caked his skin, his usual exuberance noticeably absent. "No time to explain. You have to come with me. There's something you need to see…" His face paled as he scrubbed a hand along his chin. "I... Christ, I still can't believe it."

Gabriel shook his head. "We're busy."

Greyson glanced at Uriel. "With what? Him?" The man snorted. "Please, he's not going to tell you anything. I've been listening for the last few minutes. Waiting for a good time to cut in, but..." He cupped Gabriel's arm with his other hand. "This is more important."

"Than saving mankind?"

"That's the point. It's the key." He motioned to Uriel. "Will that fire hold him?"

"Seven days."

"Can he contact his angel squad?"

Gabriel grinned. Kei's friend certainly had a way about him. "No. The fire cuts him off completely. Nothing until it releases him."

"Good, then hold on."

Kei grabbed Gabriel's hand. "Damn it, Greyson, I don't think..."

CHAPTER FIFTEEN

"Fuck, Greyson, would you stop doing that!" Kei swayed against Gabe as his balance shifted, his stomach feeling as if it'd climbed into his throat.

Greyson huffed. "You're a mage. I'd have thought you'd have gotten used to phase shifting by now."

"Not the way you do it. It's like being flung forward on a string only to be yanked back. You need to learn some finesse."

"I'll be sure to get right on that, chum." Greyson headed for the door of his home. "Are you coming?"

Kei glared at the man, taking Gabe's arm. "Are you okay?"

Gabe nodded, though Kei sensed the man's pain. Whether physical or emotional, Kei wasn't sure, but he doubted it would ease up anytime soon. He gave Gabe a smile, holding the angel's hand as he followed Greyson outside, quickly weaving their way through the glen toward an older part of the glade. Though Kei hadn't been that way in years, he recognized the markings of the Elders as they crossed into the sacred lands.

Greyson veered to his right, climbing a short rise before stopping at what looked like an oversized tree. He glanced back at them then pushed aside a hidden door amidst the bark, ducking into a narrow tunnel. Kei followed, still holding Gabe's hand as they emerged into a large room on the other side. Moonlight streamed through translucent panels in the ceiling, the walls covered in what appeared to be vines.

A man sat at a table near the back, long silver hair flowing about his shoulders. He looked up, his light-green eyes making him appear far younger than Kei suspected he was. He motioned them over, waving at the seats on the other side. Greyson plopped into one, kicking out the other two.

Kei held Gabe's, giving him a hardened look when the man frowned. "Please. I can feel how weakened you are. I know the amount of power it took to block his attack from killing me."

Gabe squeezed his hand. "Half of it was yours to begin with."

Kei winked at him, taking his place as he faced the older fae. The man seemed overly preoccupied with Gabriel, the fae's gaze pinned on Gabe.

Gabriel smiled, bowing his head slightly. "Oberon."

The man grinned, copying Gabe's action. "Gabriel. I have to admit. I never thought I'd meet an archangel in the flesh. At least, not in my realm."

"Nor I the King of the Faeries. I only wish it were under more ideal circumstances. I hope any damage my brother did was…minimal."

Oberon waved his hand. "I'm afraid his power wasn't quite what he'd hoped for while in our land. I hear you've managed to trap him."

"Temporarily." Gabriel leaned forward. "Greyson said you have something important to share with us."

"Aye. My son took it upon himself to seek answers for why the one you call Abaddon would want to imprison Michael, when he could have easily had him suffer your fate." Oberon's gaze swung to Kei. "Though, he obviously didn't count on a fire mage pulling you out of the sky before you fell. Makes me wonder if perhaps a higher power was at work."

Kei frowned. "Are you suggesting that...God..." He shook his head as he glanced up then back. "No. How?"

Oberon chuckled, nodding at Gabriel. "I see he hasn't quite come to terms with what it means to be fated to an archangel."

Gabriel grinned. "I'm easing him into it. Now, you were saying..."

Oberon nodded. "Why hasn't Abaddon simply killed Michael or cast him out? If his allies are strong enough to imprison him..."

Kei huffed. "It's because he needs Michael. We just don't know what for."

Oberon's expression saddened. "I'm afraid we do."

He motioned to an aged piece of paper. Greyson turned it around, smoothing it out before placing it in front of Kei and Gabe.

Kei stared at the lines, cursing. "Do I even want to know what language this is?"

Greyson shrugged. "It's been translated into Elvish. I

believe the original text was some kind of demonic script."

"Elvish from demonic?"

"They're a curious race. Do you want to know what it says or not?"

"You can read Elvish?"

Greyson merely cocked his head to the side.

"Of course you can." Kei held up his hand. "Sorry. It's been a long couple of days. Please...enlighten us."

Greyson trailed his finger along some of the symbols. "This section is the part you're familiar with. Stealing souls from demons so you can drain those from higher beings." He popped down a few lines. "This refers to the number of souls he needs before he can make the final sacrifice and absorb the power. Six hundred and sixty-six, in case you were wondering."

"Shit. Has he seriously killed that many?"

"Bastard's good at something, it seems."

Kei glanced at Gabriel. "So that's it? He's won?"

Greyson shook his head. "Not quite. Seems there's more to the ritual than we knew. A part I haven't seen before in any of the tellings. It says that in order to unlock the power of the warrior angels, he needs the blood of the first. He has to offer it as payment in the place of his exile on the night of the demons. Only then can Abaddon claim his prize."

Gabriel pushed to his feet, knocking the chair to the floor. "The blood of the first? He needs Michael's blood?"

Grey nodded. "I'm sorry, but it appears that way. The final offering."

Kei stood beside Gabe, reaching for his hand. "Look at

it this way. It means Michael's still alive and will be until he's needed. That gives us time."

Gabe turned to face him. "Time to do what? I don't have access to my grace unless I drain your power and even then...I can't control it."

"You don't have to drain it, I'll give it to you, and you've been getting better. You stopped Uriel from killing me, remember?"

"Putting up a barrier and fighting Orifiel and Abaddon aren't quite on the same level. Uriel was correct. If we hadn't trapped him, he would have won."

"We don't have to defeat them. Just last long enough to free your brother." Kei grinned. "Something tells me Michael will be more than a match for them. And maybe he can heal you. Unweave our powers."

Oberon coughed, gaining their attention. "You haven't told him, Gabriel?"

Kei glanced from Gabe to Oberon then back. "Told me what?"

Gabriel sighed. "I have no way of knowing whether my suspicions are true until the quest is over, and the spell is broken."

Kei grabbed Gabe. "Gabriel..."

Gabriel cupped his cheek. "There's a chance our powers will always be linked."

Kei gawked at him. "But...I thought you said it was only until we'd finished the quest? With me alive or dead."

"That was before I'd realized what Uriel had done. In casting me out... You more than saved my life, Kei. You saved my grace. But there's always a price. By denying the inevitable fall..."

"You had to give up something in return." He glanced away. "Fuck."

Oberon stood, rounding the table to stand beside them. "Gabriel will learn how to control his power, with time. How to share it with you. Nothing is lost, Kei."

Kei looked at the man—shit, the king. Just another thing he'd have to chat to Greyson about. All this time, his buddy was a prince, yet never mentioned it. "I'd just hoped that it was temporary. I promised I'd fix it. Undo what I'd unknowingly done."

"You saved him. I'll wager that trumps any... inconveniences this might cause."

"If you consider death merely an *inconvenience*, then yes."

Oberon clapped him on the shoulder. "I always did like your sense of humor. My son chose wisely when he called you friend." He motioned to the chairs, righting the one Gabe had knocked over. "Sit. We still have much to discuss."

Kei cursed under his breath. Christ, this was insane. Not that he minded being bound to Gabe. But knowing Gabriel would never be who he was before...

Gabriel placed his hand over Kei's. "I'll be far more. Now, stop worrying about my grace, and let's figure out how to stop this. Or none of that will matter."

Greyson leaned forward. "You two done?"

Kei punched his friend lightly in the shoulder. "You're still an ass. But yes."

Grey smiled. "Good, because we need to figure out the rest of it. Hard to save Michael if you don't know where the ritual's going to take place or when."

Kei snorted. "The when's easy. It says the night of the

demons. That's got to be Samhain, which is... Damn. Tomorrow."

"Which means we'd better know where to strike." He tapped a finger against his lips. "The place of his exile..." He looked over at Gabe. "Any ideas, angel-boy?"

Gabriel raked a hand through his hair. "Assuming it's referring to his exile from Heaven... I only wish I knew. No one's privy to where an angel lands after he's been cast out. That burden rests with the individual. A reflection of their crimes against Heaven. It often determines whether the fallen lives or dies."

Kei inhaled. "So...it's the place where he fell?"

Gabe nodded. "That would be my guess, though it makes sense. In order to regain entry to Heaven, he must rise from where he lost his grace."

Kei smiled. "The racetrack."

Gabe frowned. "Excuse me?"

"It's a plateau in Death Valley. Nasty place. Very fitting of his character if you ask me. But that's where he landed."

"How do you know?"

"Because the bastard told me...sort of. When he realized he couldn't drain my soul, he said he was going to banish me to the same hellhole he'd woken in. And that's where he sent me. It can't be a coincidence."

Greyson whistled. "That explains why he wanted you dead so badly. You're the one person who knows his endgame. But it also sucks. That place is wide open. Not many places to pop in without announcing yourself."

Kei shrugged. "Like I said. We only need to last long enough to release Michael."

Gabriel stood again. "We should go. Now."

Kei rose beside him, snagging his wrist as he turned toward the door. "Easy, buddy. My gut's telling me Abaddon isn't there yet. That he wouldn't risk being discovered in the only place he can perform the ritual until it's time. I'm thinking he'll flash in there tomorrow after sunset—the start of Samhain."

Gabe furrowed his brow. "Which gives us time to prepare."

"You need to rest. We *both* need to rest. At least for a few hours."

Oberon nodded. "The mage is correct. Stay. Greyson will see you get where you need to go when it's time. Until then...consider yourselves guests."

The fae waved his hand, and Kei blinked, cursing when he realized they were back in Greyson's home.

He grunted. "I really wish you'd all stop doing that. Disconcerting as hell."

Greyson slapped him on the back. "Look at it this way. He considers you part of the family, now." He leaned in close. "Did you look through that book?" His voice was hushed, barely even a whisper.

Kei gave the man a curt nod.

Grey responded in kind, straightening as he waved at the room. "Go on. Make yourselves at home. I've got some errands to run. Theories to test. I'll bunk with a friend. Let you two have some...alone time before the end of the world and all that. Give you a chance to ...recharge."

"Greyson..."

The fae smiled. "I'll be back tomorrow. Make sure you're both presentable then. Not sure my eyes could handle seeing the two of you rutting against the wall again."

"Again? Greyson?"

He vanished in a flash of blue light, his melodious chuckle echoing through the room. Kei gritted his teeth. The man needed a good ass kicking.

Kei exhaled as Gabriel's hand smoothed up his chest, tugging Kei against him. His wings brushed along Kei's sides, the soft touch making him hum. He leaned into Gabe, allowing the man to brace some of his weight.

"What a mess." He glanced back at Gabe. "You could have told me you suspected I'd screwed your power forever."

Gabe's mouth lifted into a stunning smile. "You saved me. In more ways than one. And you seem to be forgetting something."

"Which is?"

"Your magic is also bound to me."

"Pretty sure my magic doesn't compare to your grace. But if I have to share with anyone...I'd choose you."

Gabriel cupped Kei's chin, holding him steady as Gabe claimed his mouth, his tongue slipping inside. This kiss was different. Deeper. Kei felt Gabe's power slowly wrapping around him, merging with his magic in a way that seemed more intimate. Closer.

He gave himself over to the rush of pleasure. The swirl of heat along his flesh, knowing he had no control over the tiny flames that danced along his skin then onto Gabe's. Kei's magic obviously had a mind of its own where the angel was concerned.

Gabriel nuzzled his chin as he mouthed his way down Kei's neck to his shoulder. He nipped at Kei's shirt, humming when it, and the rest of their clothes, disappeared. He continued along Kei's collarbone, his wings caressing Kei's ribs.

Kei gasped. "Damn it, Gabe, you know what your feathers do to me."

Gabriel chuckled. "Which is why I'm using them. I've discovered I want you to touch them as much as you seem to need to."

Kei's head fell against Gabe as the man skimmed his other hand along Kei's abdomen, tracing his muscles before dipping lower—teasing around the base of his cock. It responded, hardening against the man's fingertips, rising out, stiff and needy from between his legs.

"Looks like I've got your full attention." Gabriel traced the length of his erection, swirling the bead of fluid around the tip.

"When don't you?" Kei hissed out a few breaths. "Not this time, Gabe. I need…"

How did he explain the crushing desire to possess Gabriel? The burning ache beneath his flesh to feel Gabriel's give around him. To have the angel surrender to him one more time.

Gabe sucked at his earlobe, leaving it with a light bite. "I'm already yours. Completely. But if you need to have me show you again…" He spun Kei in his arms, using a hand in Kei's hair to keep him anchored. "Just tell me where. The bed? The wall?" He tipped Kei's head back, placing a sucking kiss on his neck before hovering an inch away. "Here?"

"No rushing. I want to fucking taste you, first."

"What you do to me…" He released his hold, taking a single step back. "You're in control…for now."

Kei smiled at the wicked gleam in Gabe's eyes. He

loved that the angel had a playful dark side to him. That he wasn't afraid to show it to Kei.

Gabe chuckled. "You can't have light without darkness. Purity without sin. It's the choice to stay in the light that counts."

"Interesting. But all I care about right now is getting your cock in my mouth."

Kei closed the distance, claiming Gabe's lips in a desperate kiss. Gabe responded in kind, his breath raking over Kei's cheek when he finally released the angel. Gabriel held his gaze as Kei went to his knees, licking his way down Gabe's torso. Muscles contracted in sequence beneath his flesh, the sheer strength in them making Kei dizzy. The man was just too magnificent. A perfect blend of power and composure.

Images of what they'd face teased the edges of Kei's consciousness—a reminder of what he had to lose. What he needed to save. He let them hover at the far reaches of his mind, spur him to put everything he had into this pairing. Show Gabriel the true depth of his love.

Gabe muttered something above him, the words lost to a moan as Kei licked the length of the man's shaft, laving at the head. Gabe's sweet essence burst on Kei's tongue, the pureness of the flavor a testament to the man. Kei made another pass, sucking at Gabe's skin this time. The angel speared his fingers through Kei's hair, once again anchoring them together.

Gabe's thighs tensed, his head tipping back as Kei took him deep, swallowing as much of the man's length as he could. Kei kept his focus locked on Gabriel, choosing his next action by Gabe's response. By the way the muscles in his neck corded, or how his nipples beaded hard on his chest. Kei could chart the man's increasing arousal. Watching the flex and release of his arms and abdomen as he gave himself over to the pleasure.

Kei took his time, taking Gabe in then slowly withdrawing—pausing to dip between the man's legs. Suck on his sac. Gabe grunted, his hips bucking forward before he seemed to regain control. His legs stiffened, as if he were using their strength to hold himself in check.

Kei licked his way back up Gabe's length, nipping gently at the head. "I don't want you tame, Gabriel. I want the archangel in you. The side that takes what it wants, no matter the cost. I want you to lose that precious control of yours."

Gabe growled above him, the hand in his hair tightening as he dropped the other to Kei's mouth—tracing where his cock disappeared between Kei's lips. Kei upped his pace, determined to see Gabriel shatter.

Gabriel's breath rasped as he inhaled, his jaw clenching as his mouth pinched tight. His gaze held Kei's, the blue in his eyes nothing but a thin ring around the black. Kei knew the moment he surrendered. His head bowed forward as his shoulders slumped slightly, an almost painful sigh whispering between them.

He started thrusting, meeting each pass of Kei's mouth with increasing force. His metered strokes became harder, more erratic as his chest heaved from the exertion. His grip firmed, his balls pulling snug against his body.

"I can't..." His voice roughened. "Now, Kei. Yes."

His head flung back, his wings stretching then retracting as his hips punched forward, the head of his cock swelling. Kei kept moving, cupping his balls as he sucked even harder, waiting for the moment when Gabe exploded. The angel managed three more jerking thrusts before he shouted Kei's name, his release coating Kei's tongue.

He swallowed, coaxing a few more rounds out of Gabe before the man slumped over him, his wings brushing Kei's back. Kei kept him deep, savoring the last few moments of Gabe's orgasm before slowly drawing away. He planted a kiss on Gabe's hip, hissing out a breath as the man's feathers teased his skin as he rose, taking Gabe in a firm embrace.

The man's heart thrashed against Kei's ribs, the frenzied rhythm making Kei smile. Call it cocky, but he enjoyed making the angel unravel. Pushing him to the limits then watching him fall over.

Gabe tsked. "You might want to curb some of those thoughts. You're not the only one who enjoys pushing the limits."

"So not a threat, buddy." He leaned in, nipping at Gabe's lower lip. "Now that I can think remotely straight...turn around."

CHAPTER SIXTEEN

Gabriel stilled, the authoritative tone to Kei's voice triggering a similar response in him. He pushed against Kei's hand as the man palmed his chest, leaning in close. "Kei..."

Kei tsked. "My turn, Gabriel. And I don't plan on backing down. Now. Turn. Around."

Gabriel's skin warmed at the way Kei drew out his full name—one of the rare times he'd used it. Only Kei had ever shortened it. Though Gabriel had to admit, he liked it. Liked the easy way Kei accepted who and what Gabriel was without being intimidated. Without feeling the need to bow before him.

Kei chuckled. "I prefer to kneel before you...like I just did. Are we going to have to go a few rounds—have some kind of magic showdown—or are you going to trust me? And turn the fuck around. Pretty damn sure you'll enjoy giving up that control you cherish. You did last time."

Gabriel studied Kei—his lover. His true one. He couldn't ask for a stronger partner. A more worthy mate.

He released a slow breath, running his gaze the length of the other man before slowly spinning around.

Kei hummed his approval, skimming his hands over Gabriel's buttocks then up his back, tracing where his wings fused with his skin. "I still don't know what it is about your wings. Maybe it's the fact only I get to touch them. Maybe it's because of what they represent. Either way…"

He smoothed his fingertips along the edge, outlining some of Gabriel's feathers before resting them on his back again. "God, I love you."

Gabriel's heart skipped, slamming into a shaky rhythm as he glanced at Kei over his shoulder. Honesty gleamed in the man's eyes as he dipped forward and took Gabriel's mouth in his. The kiss was loving. Intimate. As if Kei had channeled his emotions into the simple act.

Gabriel tangled his fingers in Kei's hair, preventing the man from retreating. "I love you, too. Now show me."

He released his grip, allowing his head to fall against Kei as the man settled behind him. Gabriel spread out his wings, urging Kei closer before closing them around the man—holding him tightly against him.

Kei moaned. "Christ, if you're going to cocoon me with those damn wings…I won't last long."

"Neither will I."

"Shit."

Kei wrapped his arms around Gabriel, one hand collaring his neck, while the other twisted behind his head, Kei's fingers locking in Gabriel's hair. He muttered familiar words, his skin glowing a deep red. Gabriel placed one of his hands over Kei's arms, anchoring them together as a cool sensation brushed across his ass. He wondered if

Kei would insist on teasing him when the man's cock nudged Gabriel's pucker, silently demanding entrance.

He slowly exhaled, moaning as Kei increased the pressure, hovering on the edge before slipping inside, claiming the first few inches of Gabriel's channel. The resulting burn stole his breath as the mage gradually sank farther, not pausing until his balls slapped Gabriel's skin.

Kei panted against Gabriel's ear. "Fuck, do you know how incredible you feel? Hot. Tight. So damn good." Kei's forehead connected with Gabriel's shoulder. "I could lose myself in you and never care if I got found." He eased out, stopping for a few heartbeats before pushing back in. "God, Gabriel."

The man's breath caressed Gabriel's skin, cooling the overly hot feeling. All it took was one touch, and he was undone. He breathed through the next stroke, head tipping back as Kei added a bit more force, making Gabriel's body flex to absorb the shock.

Kei bit at Gabriel's neck, licking at the slight hurt. "Don't you dare hold back on me. You know what I need, Gabe."

Kei tugged on the strands fisted around his fingers as he slammed against Gabriel. Kei's other hand closed slightly around Gabriel's neck, holding him in place as Kei pounded into him, each thrust more powerful than the last. Kei's magic prickled Gabriel's skin, joining with his energy until it pulsed around them, thickening the air as it snapped and popped.

Gabriel stayed firm, chest heaving, body tense, until Kei bit at the muscle threading into Gabriel's neck, pushing him over the edge. He shouted Kei's name, releasing whatever hold he had on his control as it shattered around him—sparking like fireflies throughout the room. Tables and chairs shook as their combined power soared outward, casting a bright, orange glow throughout the space. Pleasure shot along Gabriel's nerves, stealing the last of his resolve. He came, body convulsing, head thrown back against Kei as heat enveloped his torso, slowly pulling him under.

"Fuck, yeah. That's what I want."

Kei stiffened behind him, hips jerking against Gabriel's ass as he emptied inside him, Kei's seed easing out to coat their skin. Kei's breath raked over Gabriel's shoulder as the man's head fell against him. Kei's hold loosened, the hand at Gabriel's neck dropping to palm Gabriel's chest. His heart thrashed against the mage's fingers, Kei's pulse echoing inside his head.

Kei moaned. "A millennium, huh? Might be long enough to finally slake a bit of this hunger for you, because damn... I feel as if I'll never get enough. Never love you long enough. Hold you tight enough." He dropped a kiss on neck. "Tell me you're mine."

Gabriel laughed. "Possessive streak, I see."

"Gabe..."

"Yours, Kei. And you're mine. Bound far more than any spell could achieve. I promise you that."

A shiver worked through Kei, the small tremors clenching Gabriel's heart. He gently untangled their bodies, turning to take the sorcerer in his arms, still encasing him within his wings. Kei rested his head on Gabriel's shoulder, the simple act filling Gabriel with hope. Despite everything, the man believed in him. His faith seemingly absolute. Gabriel closed his eyes, silently vowing to do all he could to be worthy of Kei's trust.

Kei sighed, lifting his head. "You could never fail me. And my faith *is* absolute. As is my love. So stop worrying, and let's end this."

Gabriel arched a brow as he did a sweep of Kei's body. "You might want to get dressed, first."

"Funny. Real funny. First, we rest. Then, come morning, we kick Abaddon's ass. Deal?"

"Deal."

Kei eased back, offering his hand before leading them to the lounge they'd stayed on before. He motioned Gabriel in, settling in front of him as he'd done before.

Gabriel chuckled. "You just like having my wings over you."

"Guilty as charged. Though I like so much more than just that. Sleep. We're going to need it."

He closed his eyes, allowing Kei's heartbeat to lull him to sleep, praying this wasn't the last time he'd feel the man next to him. Images flashed in the darkness, memories of the last battle among the angels keeping him poised on the edge of consciousness. He was just getting to the bloodiest part when a hand shook his shoulder. He bolted upright, blinking Greyson into focus.

The man tsked. "You'd think that between your combined power, one of you would have conjured up a blanket, or thought to at least put on your pants."

"Damn it, Greyson." Kei muttered a few words, covering them both in clothes before he pushed onto one elbow. "Have you heard of knocking?"

Greyson crossed his arms over his chest. "Don't blame me because you two lack forethought."

"Then don't get pissy when you walk in on something you didn't expect."

"Both of you naked is actually quite tame. I expected one of you to be pinned to something."

Kei groaned, scrubbing his hand down his face as he collapsed on the bed. "Is it sunrise already?"

Greyson sighed. "Actually, it's nearly sunset."

"What?" Kei bolted up, almost tumbling off the small lounge. "Why didn't you wake us? Abaddon—"

"Isn't there, yet." Greyson held up his hand at Kei's arched brow. "My father noticed how drained you both were. Knowing what you'd be facing... He decided to send a small group of his warriors to survey the place. Turns out, it's been sealed with wards..." Greyson whistled again. "Talk about old school. I've never seen anything like them."

Gabriel grunted. "Orifiel."

Greyson shrugged. "Doesn't really matter. It's impenetrable."

"If my brother constructed the seals, I can break them."

"But I'm guessing he'd know, right?" Greyson shrugged as they gained their feet. "Not sure which is worse... Facing Abaddon and his crew when they don't know you're coming, or when they do. If you wait until they appear—break the wards, themselves—at least you'll still have the element of surprise."

Gabriel mulled it over, hating that the fae's logic seemed sound. They couldn't afford to alert Abaddon that they knew where the ritual would take place. He'd only assemble an even greater force.

He nodded at Greyson. "How will we know when they've arrived?"

"One of my brothers stayed behind. He'll summon us

when your friends get there."

Kei stepped forward. "Us?"

Greyson snorted. "I'm coming with you."

Kei shook his head. "This isn't your fight."

"No. It's everyone's fight. Come on, Kei. If Abaddon succeeds in completing that ritual, how long do you think my realm will survive before he decimates it? We're a strong race, but against power that absolute?" He blew out a slow breath. "Even we would fall, eventually. I can't let that happen. Not without doing all I can." He waved Kei off. "I'm not asking. So make peace with it."

Kei glanced at Gabriel, his expression softening. He crossed over to Greyson, taking the man's forearm in his. "Thank you."

Greyson slapped Kei on the shoulder. "You're welcome. Now, can we stop with all the touchy feely crap? I've seen where it leads with you."

Kei gave the man a shove, turning to face Gabriel. "You ready?"

He nodded, knowing his voice would sound hollow if he replied. Kei cupped his shoulder, giving him an encouraging smile. Gabriel didn't deserve the other man's undying faith, but he'd take it. Kei tsked, moving in closer when the air crackled, a bright, green flash filling the room. A man materialized out of the light, quickly heading for Greyson.

He stopped in front of the fae, eyes wide, hair wild about his head. "They just arrived."

Greyson clapped the man on the back. "How many?"

The other fae frowned. "Only a handful of demons, and a man incased in fire. But..." He looked over at Gabriel. "There's one like him, only..." He swallowed. "I've never felt that much raw power other than from Father. He's dangerous, Greyson."

"They aren't the only ones with an archangel on their side. Now, go tell Father. I'll take Kei and Gabriel down."

The man inhaled sharply, pursing his lips before winking out again.

Greyson walked over to them. "Looks like it's party time. Here, take this."

Greyson waved his hand, muttering some words before a sword appeared in his palm. He smiled, holding it out to Kei. "I know you prefer to use your fire, but... Never hurts to have a good sword at your side."

Kei accepted the offering, turning the weapon over in his hands. "Not sure what you all see in these, but... Thank you."

Greyson cocked his head to the side. "You do know how to wield one of those, right?"

"Ass. Of course, I do. I just prefer to use my magic. Spells and fire are far more pure. Not to mention less messy."

"Have it your way." Greyson glanced at Gabriel. "What about you, angel-boy? You need a sword?"

Gabriel resisted rolling his eyes. "I'm fine."

Kei grabbed Greyson's arm. "Trust me, he's got his own weapon, which you'll see later. Whenever you're ready, Grey."

Greyson drew a deep breath, his blue light swirling around them. He muttered more words, the telltale shift making Gabriel's breath hitch. He held onto Kei, jaw clenched tight, muscles primed for battle, when the light dissipated into darkness. He blinked, allowing his eyes to adjust to the hazy moonlight peeking above the distant rocks. The air crackled around them, his brother's power prickling the hairs on his arm.

He turned to Kei. "Orifiel's here. I feel his grace."

Kei nodded. "What about Michael?"

"He's...cut off."

"Most likely that damn blood fire." Kei cursed under his breath. "And it looks like we have company."

Gabriel spun, watching as a line of demons headed toward them. But Greyson's brother had been right. There were far fewer than Gabriel had anticipated.

Kei snorted. "He has an archangel in his ranks. He doesn't need a demon army. Not to mention the fact he probably never thought we'd ever make it this far." Kei stepped in front of Gabriel, holding him back with his arm. "I'll take care of the demons. You save your strength. You're the only here who stands a chance against Orifiel."

Gabriel tamped down his frustration, muttering as Kei ran toward the line, skin gleaming red in the darkness. Bursts of flames brightened the night as the mage launched multiple attacks, systematically destroying the creatures. Pride swelled inside Gabriel's chest as his mate downed the last of the horde, his magic still surrounding him in a crimson glow.

Gabriel headed over to him, Greyson in tow. "I'll never tire of seeing the warrior in you. Though, I'd prefer that it wasn't necessary."

Kei smiled, but Gabriel felt the weakness already creeping into Kei's body. "Demons are easy in comparison to what lies ahead." He cupped Gabriel's shoulder. "Are you sure you're up to this? Facing your brother?"

"Michael is our only concern. As for Orifiel... He's already chosen his path. He's beyond my help."

"Then, let's go. I sense Abaddon. He's on the other side of that outcrop. While I realize they're already aware of our presence...once we crossover..."

"There's no turning back." Gabriel placed his hand at his hip, slowly exhaling as his sword flashed to life, the familiar weight of it banishing the last of his doubts. He raised it to his chest, watching how the moonlight gleamed on the inscription carved into the hilt.

The bearer shall stand against the darkness, and wage battle against the forces of evil. For without sacrifice, there is no glory.

He glanced at his friends, giving them one final nod. Live or die, he'd make his stand.

CHAPTER SEVENTEEN

Kei reined in his magic, caging it just below the surface. The familiar warmth grounded him. Gave him focus. He glanced at Greyson. Shit, he still couldn't believe the man had volunteered to join them. Insisted, really. Not that Kei didn't welcome the added strength. He just didn't want to be the reason yet another of his friends died. He'd failed Grey's sister. He couldn't fail Grey, too.

Gabriel glanced over at him, his expression clearly stating he'd heard Kei's thoughts. He didn't want to fail Gabe, either, but Gabe already knew that. Even if the man hadn't been able to read his mind, Kei had shown him—in the way they'd kissed, how he'd allowed Gabe to bear some of his responsibility. And Kei had no doubts that Gabe knew how far he'd go to keep his word—save Gabe's grace.

Gabriel stopped as they approached the far side of the outcrop, turning to face them. "Are you both sure this is what you want? I can face my brother alone."

Kei merely snorted as Greyson gave Gabe a look that clearly stated he thought Gabe was crazy.

Gabe smiled, reaching for Kei then tugging him close. He didn't seem to care that Greyson was watching as he brushed his lips over Kei's. "Stick close. And don't do anything...reckless. Losing you would kill me as surely as my brother's power."

He pressed his mouth to Kei's, lingering just long enough to infuse his taste into Kei's senses before breaking away. Gabe faced front again, taking a deep breath before marching forward. "There's no point in being stealthy. They're waiting for us."

Greyson made a strangled grunting sound as they crossed onto the other side, the full length of the plateau stretching out before them. Kei kept on Gabriel's left as they headed for the altar erected near the center of the area, the raised platform illuminated by a number of torches. Shadows danced along the edge of the ring of light, the abstract patterns making the caked dirt look as if it were breathing.

A few more demons milled around them, watching but not attacking. Gabe ignored them, heading steadily toward the three silhouettes gathered within the light, their shadows stretching out toward them.

He stopped as he crossed into the glowing circle, head held high, wings folded along his back. He looked regal. Angelic. He didn't speak, just stood there, staring at the man off to Abaddon's right.

The being moved forward, golden wings stretching to either side of him. "Gabriel."

"Orifiel."

He smiled. "I knew you'd come. When Uriel

disappeared... I knew it was you. That we'd failed, yet again, to stay your faith. Did you kill him?"

Gabe looked away for a moment. "No. Even after all you've done... You. Uriel. You're still my brothers. I have no desire to take your life."

Orifiel laughed. "You always were the merciful one. Willing to see the good in everyone. Even the abominations you're trying to save. It's a shame you can't see the truth. Look beyond your misplaced faith into the heart of the monsters you risk your life for. Maybe then you'd see we're only doing what's needed. Preserving the paradise our Father truly envisioned."

Gabriel shook his head. "Can't you see? This is already paradise."

"This is Hell on Earth."

"No, brother. I'll concede. They're primitive. So much to learn, but isn't that our purpose? To guide them? Help them stay in the light? Killing them... It goes against everything Father has taught us."

"Father can't see the truth. He's blinded by His love for them. His unwavering faith. Yet, every day they slip farther into the abyss. Killing. Destroying. Mocking our very existence. They don't believe in us anymore, Gabriel. Why should we believe in them?"

"Is that why we were created? For them to cherish? Worship? They might have lost their faith in me, but I still believe in them. Even if just one soul finds solace in my presence—that's enough. It has to be enough, Orifiel."

The angel sighed as he took a step closer. "I'm not the enemy. We both want to save them. I'm just strong enough to see they can't *all* be saved. It's time to wash the slate clean. Put an end to the evil lurking among them.

Join us, brother. Help us usher in a new era of peace. Purity. All Father had hoped for. He'll thank us once we're done. We're giving Him what He's always wanted."

"Perhaps it's time we gave him what He needs, instead. And what He *needs*, is your loyalty. Your love."

A blast of light split the night as Orifiel clenched his fists, his anger rolling off him in waves. "Don't judge me. You have no idea how strong my love is. How hard it was to make the choices I have. And it's all for Him. Because of my love *for Him*."

"So killing Michael? Is that showing Father your love for Him?"

"Is that what you think? That we're going to kill Michael?" Orifiel laughed. "He's here to witness the truth. The end of darkness as we know it. Once we make the final offering...those who are unworthy will perish, leaving behind a world deserving of our love."

"Is that what Abaddon told you? If you're not going to kill Michael, what's your final sacrifice?"

"We only need a bit of his blood. To purify the offering. Activate the cleanse."

Gabe looked at the man in question. "I have to hand it to you, Abaddon. Convincing two of my brothers to abandon their faith—to blindly follow you—you're far stronger than any of us ever imagined."

Abaddon grinned. "I'm merely showing them the path to salvation."

"Your lies roll off your tongue with such ease. If only they knew your true intentions."

He snorted. "Are you sure you do? Not that long ago, your mage followed me. I saved him from the darkness, gave him purpose, and still he turned on me. He's the one who's filled your head with lies, Gabriel. The one who'll betray you."

Kei stiffened at the man's words, his magic crackling around him. He'd forgotten how convincing the man could be.

Gabriel gave Kei a stunning smile. "I've seen his soul. Felt it. It's pure—unlike yours."

Orifiel hissed, stepping forward. "Abaddon is our brother."

Gabe's power snapped at the words. "And Kei is my true one. I'll trust his soul over that of a fallen any day. Have you forgotten what Abaddon did? Why he was cast out? There are demons guarding you, Orifiel. Demons! How can you not see the truth?"

"Enough." The glow on Orifiel's skin increased. "This is your last chance, Gabriel. Join us."

"I can't. I won't abandon my faith."

"So be it."

Orifiel lifted his hands, sending a bolt of yellow light toward them. Gabriel's power answered in kind, extending in front of them in a wall of white light. Kei channeled his magic, adding it to Gabe's, praying his energy would strengthen their defense. Orifiel's ray collided with the barrier, igniting in a blaze of fire as it exploded, billowing out around them. The air crackled from the force, raising the hairs on Kei's neck. Gabriel glanced at him, but he just nodded.

"I think I'm getting the hang of sharing. Do what you must, Gabe. I've got your back."

Kei released another beam, drawing a line of flames between Abaddon and Michael's ring, cutting the man off when he tried to move toward the angel. Abaddon motioned with his hands, smiling when the demons closed in around them.

Greyson spun. "I'll take care of the demons. You two deal with the crazy angel."

The man took off, his blue light gleaming in the growing darkness. Kei focused on Orifiel, trying to read the angel's next attack by the way he moved. The man studied them, as if confused why his power hadn't simply killed them, before leaping off the platform.

He landed on the parched dirt, kicking up a small cloud of dust as he looked them in the eyes. "It didn't have to end this way."

Gabe sighed. "Then choose the light. Stop this madness."

Orifiel drew his sword, holding it out in front of him. "Oh, I will."

He attacked, his weapon slicing through the air in quick, smooth arcs. Gabriel darted in front of Kei as he parried the strikes, sparks glinting off the blades as they collided. Orifiel launched into the air, wings kicking up a spray of dust. Gabe snarled and followed, matching every move the other angel made. They clashed in mid-air, the echoing clatter of metal ringing across the plateau. Orifiel's grace glowed around him, the added power giving him an obvious advantage.

Gabriel battled back, losing ground as the fight dragged on. Kei cursed, directing his magic at Gabriel, surrendering more of his energy as he fed the other man in a steady stream of crimson light. Kei felt Gabe's grace surge forward, dosing his mate's skin in a pure, white glow. The added power seemed to even the odds, and the two angels broke apart. They descended again, both withdrawing slightly as their ragged breaths sounded around them.

Orifiel glared at him. "You always were the better swordsman. But you're weak. Even with your sorcerer's help. You won't outlast me, brother."

"Perhaps. But there's more to winning a battle than sheer strength."

"Then let's put that to the test."

He channeled his energy, hitting Gabe point blank. Gabriel shouted, his pain echoing through Kei, as his mate dropped to his knees, his head bowed to his chest. A dull ringing sounded inside Kei's head, the scenery starting to spin. He felt Gabe gather what power he had around him, obviously hoping to shield himself from the burning energy.

Kei fisted his hands, drawing on every ounce of magic he could muster. He let it flow through him, channeling it at Orifiel. The angel cried out, his energy quickly pulling back—releasing its hold on Gabriel. Kei ran to his mate, muttering a spell as he directed the healing toward Gabe. The angel inhaled, opening his eyes as the burns washed from his skin, Kei's energy slowly sinking beneath the surface.

Kei wiggled his fingers. "Take my hand."

Gabriel clasped the man's arm, levering himself up. Kei focused on Orifiel. The archangel knelt on the dirt off to their right, his chest heaving as he slowly got to his feet. Black streaks were burned across his wings, smeared blood marring his face.

Kei stood his ground as he glanced at Gabe. "You okay?"

Gabriel nodded. "How?"

"I've got a few ancient spells up my sleeve. No one's infallible, remember? But I'm not sure how long I can keep it up. He's too strong." He exhaled a shuttering breath. "You should drain me. If you free your grace completely, you might have what it takes to kick his ass."

"You'll be defenseless. Abaddon will kill you."

"None of that matters. You have to stop this or everyone's dead."

Gabe glanced at his brother, then back at Kei. "I can't sacrifice you to save myself. I'll hold Orifiel off. See if you can get to Michael."

"Gabriel, no!"

His mate took to the sky, Orifiel following behind him. Punches of light brightened the darkness as their battle continued, the echoed clang of swords filling the air. Kei gritted his teeth, preparing to channel his remaining energy at Gabriel, when Greyson grabbed his arm. Kei spun, cursing at the lacerations marring his friend's skin.

Greyson fisted his shirt, tugging Kei in close. "Surrendering your power won't be enough. You have to use the spell."

Kei shook his head. "It's madness. Even if it works... Damn it, Grey, there's no guarantee *he'll* even help us."

"If Abaddon succeeds, even *he'll* fall against the bastard's power. Have faith, Kei. It's all we've got."

Kei cursed under his breath, shoving Greyson behind him as Abaddon jumped off the platform, marching toward them. He held a sword similar to Gabe's, the silver blade glinting in the moonlight. He stopped several feet away, a twisted smile lifting his lips.

He braced his feet apart as he stared at them, ignoring the battle still raging overhead. "Kei. After all this time, it seems I'm still underestimating you. Teaming up with an archangel." He chuckled. "*That*, I didn't see coming. It's too bad your friend isn't quite as strong as mine. Falling does that to an angel."

Kei sneered at him. "I imagine you know exactly what kind of toll it takes. This is where you fell, after all."

"So it is. You know, Kei, that's my only real regret. Sending you here. It was a cocky move, I'll admit. But then in my defense, I thought sending an endless stream of demons after you would solve that problem. But what do you do?" He laughed, spreading his arms wide. "You kill every damn one of them and then...then...you summon Gabriel. My fucking brother, Gabriel! And on the eve I finally convince my brothers to cast him out. Drug his damn wine, and toss him out of Heaven." He shook a finger at Kei. "You are full of surprises. Too little, too late, mind you, but...a valiant effort."

"Gloat all you want, Abaddon, but you haven't completed the ritual, yet. And I doubt obtaining Michael's blood will be that easy. Even imprisoned, he's still a warrior."

Kei glanced at Michael, barely visible beyond the flickering blue flames of the circle holding him captive. The archangel hadn't so much as looked up, still poised on his knees, his head bowed, his hands behind his back. Even his wings seemed limp, half their length slumped on the ground. Abaddon must have had Orifiel transport the stone beneath Michael in order to keep him trapped, which didn't bode well for Gabriel. Abaddon was right. Orifiel was far stronger.

Kei swung his gaze back to Abaddon, noting the smug look on the man's face. Doubt wove down Kei's spine, and he had a bad feeling they'd missed something. That Abaddon had already sealed their fate.

The man grinned. "Do you really think I'd leave that crucial part of the ritual until the end? You know me better than that, Kei." He reached into his shirt, removing a vial filled with blood. "I'm afraid poor Michael is quite drained already. Even if you managed to release him, he's weak. Even more so than Gabriel. Looks like you're out of aces, Mage. I win."

Kei shot a blast of fire at the man, but Abaddon blocked it, the strength of the souls he'd consumed obviously increasing his power. He motioned at Kei, tossing him backwards onto the ground, his head cracking hard against the packed dirt. Black dots skirted his vision, as the scenery swam, pain sparking through his back and skull.

Greyson loomed over him, grabbing his hand and yanking him upright. The fae deflected Abaddon's next attempt, the man's blue light staining the darkness. "We're out of time. I'll keep Abaddon busy. You do the summoning."

Kei shook his head. "It's too dangerous. What if I fuck it up?"

"We're dead either way. Gabriel won't last much longer against his brother, and Abaddon just drank Michael's blood. *He's* our only chance."

"Shit! Fine. Keep moving. Abaddon's lazy when it comes to his power. Even increased, he tends to do whatever is easiest. All I need is five minutes."

Greyson hissed as a ray of blood-red light bounced off him. "I can't promise you more than two. Work fast."

The fae turned, darting off, pummeling Abaddon with

a steady stream of energy. The bastard returned fire, seemingly occupied with Greyson. Kei reached into his pocket, removing the pages he'd stuffed in earlier. He smoothed them out, holding back a near hysterical laugh as he stared at the text, the ancient spell openly mocking him. He was insane. There was no other explanation.

He grabbed the sword Greyson had given him, using the tip to slice a long line across his palm. He smeared the blood across the dirt, the dry surface nearly as hard as stone. The symbols took shape, each marking bringing him closer to the end—he just wasn't sure if it'd be Abaddon's or theirs.

He completed the sigil, double-checking each token before drizzling more blood in the center. He drew a deep breath then began reciting the verse, focusing on each syllable, allowing the words to flow off his tongue in an easy cadence. He'd reached the last line, when Greyson landed hard beside him, a huge gash marring the man's left side. Blood oozed from the wound, the edges of the fae's skin tinged black. Kei reached for him, but Greyson waved him off.

"Finish it, Kei. Now!"

Kei turned back, watching as Abaddon moved into view, the man's skin glowing an eerie shade of red. The ritual was working. Kei felt the power radiating off the man—growing in intensity with every passing breath. The bastard snarled, lifting his hands when a flash of white light exploded the ground in front of him. Gabe swooped down, landing in a billow of dust between them. Blood dripped from several wounds across his back and sides, more lacerations lining his arms.

He pushed to his feet, glancing over at Kei before

Orifiel landed next to Abaddon, the man's power still shimmering around him. Gabe looked at the sigil, eyes widening before he met Kei's gaze.

"No, Kei, you can't…"

Kei recited the last few words, offering more blood before focusing his magic. Flames raced along his arms and across his torso, covering him in a sea of fire. He gave Gabe one last smile then tipped back his head as he unleashed his power, setting the sigil alight. The symbol flared, filling the sky with a blinding red light as the blood sizzled and popped, glaring bright then slowly sinking into the earth. His energy arced across his flesh, drawing a scream from his chest as he fell forward, collapsing onto the ground. The earth shook beneath him, an echoed scream sounding across the plateau before Kei's strength waned. He closed his eyes, releasing his claim on his power as it joined with Gabe's, leaving Kei to float in the darkness, nothing but the ghostly sound of his name following him under.

CHAPTER EIGHTEEN

"Kei!"

Gabriel inhaled as Kei's magic slammed into him, knocking him onto one knee. He braced his palm on the ground, bits of crusty mud biting into his skin. He breathed through the searing heat that scorched his skin, watching as flames erupted on his flesh before slowing, swirling beneath the surface.

Power surged to life inside him, the sheer force of his grace stealing his breath. If felt as if a thousand suns had suddenly burst to life, their light blinding him. He grunted through the resulting pain, raising his gaze as the sensations finally started to pass. Abaddon stood in front of him, eyes wide, fear slashing in their depths. Orifiel seemed equally stunned, confusion shading his expression.

Gabriel gathered his strength, gaining his feet as his skin glowed like a beacon, the warm orange color a testament to his and Kei's combined strength. He looked down at his hands, smiling at the way Kei's fire seemed to curl along his skin, as if licking at it.

He glanced back at Kei. The mage had collapsed onto the dirt, eyes closed, body limp. Though he sensed Kei's heartbeat, knowing his mate had sacrificed everything for one last chance clenched his chest until simply breathing seemed to take all his energy. His heart wanted him to go to Kei—restore his power. But that wouldn't save him. Not once Abaddon unleashed his fury. Kei was safer like this. And Gabriel couldn't fail the man. Not now.

Gabriel turned toward Abaddon, holding his head high as he probed the man's strength. Though not at the level claimed by the scriptures, it had definitely increased, and Gabriel had a bad feeling that it wouldn't stop growing until it'd reached the level stated in the ancient texts. Until Abaddon rivaled God himself.

Abaddon clapped his hands as he shook his head. "Well, well, well. Yet, another surprise. So I guess this means your grace is linked to Kei somehow. He goes down —you get stronger. How interesting."

Gabe's power snapped, shooting rays into the air. He fisted his hands, doing his best to rein the energy back inside—offer up some semblance of control.

Abaddon laughed this time. "You can't control it, can you? Oh, this is so much more delicious. Orifiel…"

Orifiel took a step toward Gabriel then stopped, spinning to face Abaddon. "You made the blood offering. Why isn't the spell working?"

Abaddon sighed. "It is working. It's just not the spell you were expecting."

He struck, stabbing Orifiel in the shoulder before twisting the blade, shoving it deeper. He yanked it free, grinning as the archangel tripped onto the ground, his blood staining the dirt. Orifiel made a hushed gurgling noise before collapsing back, his body shuddering.

"No!" Gabriel moved forward only to stop when Abaddon exploded a patch of mud next to Gabriel's feet.

"Relax, Gabriel. I'm simply sparing him the anguish of watching everything he loves burn into ash. It's a shame Kei isn't awake to witness it, though. I would have loved to have watched his faith slowly die—wither like yours and Michael's will." He turned his face toward the sky, his power coloring his skin. "So this is what it feels like? To wield the Hand of God without fear of retribution? I never dreamed it'd be this satisfying."

Gabriel held his ground, grunting as his grace tried to break free—attack Abaddon of its own accord. Sweat beaded his brow, and his limbs shook at his sides. "It's not over, yet. Not until my dying breath."

"Do you really think you're a match for me? You're only half the angel you used to be."

Gabriel glanced at Michael. His brother had managed to raise his head, but the man's weakness was more than evident. He tugged at the bonds binding his hands, grimacing from the pain.

Abaddon tsked. "Michael can't save you, now. Even if you could free him, he's too weak. Like you."

"I'm strong enough to break his cage."

Gabriel directed his energy toward the ring, using his power to douse the flames—free his brother. But his attempt merely bounced off the fire, sparking into a thousand shards of light.

"I told you. You can't break it. I knew you'd turn to big brother for help, so I warded the flames. Nothing pure can break the spell, which means even your mage and your fae friend are helpless to destroy it. I'm afraid you're on your own..."

Abaddon's voice trailed off as the plateau shook, knocking them both to their knees. Gabriel braced his hand on the earth, holding tight as another tremor split the ground open, venting steam into the air. Spires of ash shot upwards, covering the dirt in gray specks before a crack of thunder broke the silence, flashes of lightning striking the mud. A scream mixed in with the rumble overhead, followed by an eerie void.

Gabriel waved his hand to clear the air, his stomach dropping as he stared at the man crouched on the ground, smoke curling off his skin, muscles flexing as he slowly gained his feet, rolling his shoulders as he turned to scan the area. His gaze locked on Gabriel's as a slow smile spread across his face.

He brushed some of the soot off his chest then crossed his arms, looking far too cocky for his own good. "Well, I'll be damned. Gabriel. Long time no see."

Gabriel swallowed past the lump in his throat. Kei had done it. He'd actually summoned his brother.

Gabriel managed to stand, nodding at the man. "Lucifer."

Lucifer placed his hand over his heart. "You remembered. I'm touched." He glanced over his shoulder. "And is that Michael? Shit, it's like a fucking family reunion." His gaze locked on Abaddon, the cheery disposition quickly vanishing. "And *you*. You have some explaining to do—killing my demons without asking. But first, let's gather everyone closer, shall we?"

He stretched out his arms, clenching his fists toward him—cursing when only Gabriel stumbled a few feet forward, the fallen angel's power warring with Gabriel's unstable energy. Lucifer frowned, repeating the action, arching a brow when only Gabriel moved again.

Gabriel grunted, catching his balance. "Would you stop doing that? He performed the ancient soul ritual. Your power has no effect on him."

Lucifer glanced at Abaddon then back to Gabriel. "You don't say. Then who the hell summoned me? Which was a fucking ballsy move, if I do say so. They're lucky I didn't disintegrate their damn soul in the process."

Abaddon laughed, slowly walking forward. "The fire mage thought he'd pull a rabbit out of his hat. A last ditch effort to best me, I assume. Too bad even your power doesn't compare to mine. Not anymore."

Lucifer ignored Abaddon, looking at Gabriel. "You let a fire mage summon me?"

Gabriel shrugged. "Kei's...stubborn."

Lucifer stared between him and Kei, grinning. "Well, fuck. I sense his magic woven through your grace, which seems a bit out of control, bro. You might want to rein it in..." He paused, then laughed. "Dear God, you're bound to him, aren't you?"

"Thinking that's not what's important here. Did you miss the part where I told you Abaddon's completed the soul ritual?"

"Nah, I heard that. I just don't give a shit." He scowled. "What? The man's crazy." He turned to Abaddon. "Sorry, but it's true. Especially if you think this will work out the way you intended."

Abaddon growled, releasing a blast of power, sending chunks of mud bursting into the air. "I'll see you bow before me."

Lucifer chuckled. "Sure." He turned to Gabriel. "He does know that having power and actually wielding it are completely different, right? Because I'm betting he couldn't hit us if he tried."

Gabriel shook his head. "Lucifer, I wouldn't…"

Abaddon lashed out, sending a bolt toward them. It missed high, sailing over them—exploding on the other side of the plateau. The man cursed, making another attempt, only to miss again.

Lucifer tsked, cocking his head to the side as he sent a blast of fire at Abaddon. The blow knocked him backwards, but quickly dissipated, sending more ash into the air. Lucifer frowned, trying again, cursing when his flames sputtered out as they hit some kind of invisible force.

Gabriel joined the other man, motioning toward Abaddon. Gabriel channeled his power with Lucifer's, Gabriel's shoulders slumping when all it did was knock the man back farther.

Abaddon grinned then attacked. Gabriel directed his energy into the ground, raising a barrier of stone, deflecting the blast before it hit. He erected a second wall, using his power to drag Orifiel, Kei and Greyson behind it. Hoping to at least shield them from some of Abaddon's energy.

"Shit!" Lucifer gazed at Gabriel. "Why the hell didn't you summon me *before* he finished the damn ritual? I'm not much use, now."

Gabriel glared at the man. "I was a bit busy trying to stay alive. And we both know, I never would have summoned you."

"Then you're an ass. Hell might not be much, but it's

mine. And I don't like it when someone tries to take what's mine." He peeked around the edge, sending another blaze of fire out. "What the hell's wrong with Michael? Why hasn't he gone all warrior ninja on Abaddon's ass? This is right up his alley."

"Blood fire. And Abaddon warded it. Nothing pure can break through."

Lucifer laughed. "You don't say…"

He moved past Gabriel, lining up Michael's cage before releasing a single finger of power at the flames. The blue light hissed then flared, flickering wildly before winking out. Michael raised his head, spreading his wings before taking to the sky, disappearing into the darkness. The air fluttered around them a moment before Michael crashed to the ground behind them, muscles clenched tight as he managed to stumble to his feet.

Gabriel caught him when he swayed sideways, shouldering most of his weight. "You're weak. You need to rest."

Michael waved him off. "What I need is to lock up Abaddon's ass for the next millennia." He slumped against Gabriel.

Gabriel sighed. "You'll be lucky not to pass out." He furrowed his brow. "I could try healing you, but…"

Lucifer stepped forward. "Oh for fuck's sake. You'll kill him, your damn grace is so out of control. Here." He cupped Michael's face, sending a bolt of energy through him, nearly knocking him on his ass before Gabriel tightened his grip. "But I swear, if you ever…ever… mention this…"

Michael huffed, rolling his shoulders as he straightened. "You think I like this?" He exhaled as another blast hit the barrier. "Even with three of us... I'm not sure it'll be enough."

Lucifer sighed. "Doesn't anyone study the ancient scrolls except me? Even though Abaddon's completed the ritual, it doesn't grant him infinite power instantly. The power comes from the souls he's consumed, which means it has to work its way through them. All six-hundred and sixty-six. Until that happens, he's vulnerable to any spell that would work on us."

Gabriel turned. "So we can imprison him in blood fire or trap him with a sigil?"

"Those are only temporary. He'd bust free once he gained enough strength. If we want stop him, we'll have to banish him somewhere he won't be able to access that power."

Michael scoffed. "Where's that?"

Lucifer glared at him. "Hey, I did my part. You're supposed to be all knowing, *brother*."

"Enough." Gabriel wedged between them. "Fighting amongst ourselves isn't going to solve this. You two can go at it once Abaddon's gone, but until then..." He reran Lucifer's words in his head. "A spell."

Lucifer shoved him. "What the hell are you talking about now?"

"You said we had to banish him. That requires a spell."

Michael nodded toward Kei. "Your mage."

Gabriel snagged Michael's wrist. "I'll restore his power, but I'll lose access to my grace. I'll still stand with you, but..."

"But you'll be weak." Lucifer shook his head. "This just keeps getting better. Well, fuck it. Do what you need.

I'm tired of standing behind this hunk of rock. And Abaddon's pissed me off."

Michael hissed as Lucifer stepped out, sending waves of fire through the air. "I can't believe it's come to this. To...*him*." He motioned to Kei. "Do what you must, brother. I'll hit Abaddon with all I have."

Gabriel nodded, offering Michael his sword. "Abaddon has yours."

Michael accepted the blade. "Then it's time I got it back."

He launched into the air, disappearing once again. Gabriel drew a deep breath, adding his power to the fight as he made his way over to Kei, kneeling beside the man. His face was balled into a grimace, his hand still leaking blood onto the ground.

Gabriel brushed Kei's hair back, allowing a trickle of power to move between them. Kei groaned, blinking a few times before opening his eyes. Stunning green looked up at Gabriel, confusion clouding over them.

Kei glanced around, groaning when he tried to move. "Gabe?"

"Easy. You took quite a blow with that spell."

He moistened his lips. "Did it work?"

Gabriel snorted. "What made you think summoning Lucifer was a good idea? Where did you even get the spell?"

"Did it work?"

"He's as annoying as ever, but yes...unfortunately, even he's no match for Abaddon. He and Michael—"

"They're fighting together? On the same side? Now that I'll have to see for myself." He tried to sit up only to fall back down. "Damn."

"We're running out of time. Lucifer seems to think the only way to stop Abaddon is to banish him somewhere he doesn't have access to the power." He shook his head. "I'm not sure I understand what he means…"

Kei frowned. "I'm sorry, Gabe, but there's no realm that would cut him off. Not completely."

"Kei. The book."

Gabriel turned as Greyson's voice sounded beside them. The fae had pushed onto one elbow, an old leather tome extended toward them. Gabriel took the offering, handing it to Kei as Greyson collapsed, his eyes drifting shut.

Gabriel clenched his jaw. He hated not having control. Being unable to do the simplest of acts.

Kei punched him in the shoulder. "We can save Greyson after. If there is an after. Now help me up."

Gabriel wrapped his arm around Kei, jumping when rocks and mud exploded nearby, spraying them with chunks. The air thickened a moment before Lucifer landed in a heap by their feet, smoke rising up from his flesh.

He groaned, rolling onto his hands and knees as he shook his head. He glanced at Gabriel. "Damn that hurt. Bastard will pay for that one. Hurry up and find a way to banish him. We're getting our asses kicked."

He unleashed a wall of fire as he headed back toward the fight, the air crackling around them.

Kei stared after the man, eyes wide. "That's Lucifer?" He snorted. "Not what I expected."

Gabriel couldn't help but grin as Kei flipped through the pages, skimming each spell. "I know. He's quite beautiful."

"Minus the whole evil thing."

Kei kept turning, his shoulders drooping a bit more as he neared the end of the book. He shook his head, getting to the last spell when he stopped, his breath catching. He scanned through the verses, muttering to himself before looking up at Gabriel. "This could work."

"What is it?"

"Might be better if you don't know. You thought summoning Lucifer was crazy, but this…"

He maneuvered onto his hands and knees, every movement drawing another grunt. Gabriel channeled more of his power, but Kei shook him off.

"I don't need it, yet." He gave Gabriel a slight shove. "Go. Help your brothers. It'll take me a few minutes to prepare the spell. But when I shout your name…hit me with everything you've got."

"Kei. If I send that much raw power at you…it could kill you, bound together or not. I simply don't have the control I need."

"Do you have any idea what I'm about to do?" He waved off Gabriel's arched brow. "Forget it, just…trust me. And hit me with all of it."

Gabriel glared at Kei, but the man shooed him away, pointing toward the battle. Gabriel stood, watching for a few more heartbeats before taking to the sky, swooping down toward Abaddon. The man was surrounded by an ungodly red glow, his power quickly absorbing any attack. Michael flew in low, striking at Abaddon with Gabriel's sword only to be struck with a finger of light. It cut through Michael's wing, careening him toward the ground.

Gabriel dove at the angel, catching him before he hit. Gabriel bridged the man's weight, carrying him behind one of the barriers before easing him onto the parched dirt. Black stained the pearl-colored feathers, the gaping hole churning Gabriel's stomach.

Michael drew a few deep breaths, bloody lines scattered across his skin. "He's getting stronger with each passing moment. I'm not sure how much longer we can hold him."

"Kei's working on a spell. We just need to buy him a few more minutes."

Michael nodded, firming his shoulders as he clenched his jaw. "Your mage will get his time."

He stretched his wings, then took off, somehow gaining altitude despite the wound. Gabriel followed after him, directing his power at Abaddon. The force of his attack knocked Gabriel back, a further testament to his lack of control. The blow barely touched the other man, simply shoving Abaddon over slightly. He turned, sending a bolt toward Gabriel.

He ducked, continuing the futile attempts until he thought his head would explode from the constant flux of his energy. He landed beside Lucifer, helping the downed man gain his feet.

Lucifer took a few stumbling steps. "Where the hell is that spell? If we wait much longer, nothing will work."

"I'm sure Kei's—"

"Gabe!"

Gabriel turned as Kei's voice rose about the crackle of power.

His mate nodded. "Now!"

Gabriel pursed his lips, staring at his hands as his grace surged forward, stealing his breath. He shook his head. He'd kill Kei.

Kei smiled. "Trust me. Now, Gabe."

Gabriel cursed, directing his power at Kei, crying out as it exploded toward the mage, hitting him full force. Kei jerked back, head tipped up, arms extended to either side before he reached toward the ground, releasing a blinding flash of red light. It struck the symbols he'd inscribed on the dirt, casting a ghostly reflection of the sigil into the sky. Thunder clapped overhead as clouds rushed together, blocking out the moonlight.

Kei's body shook, his limbs blazing with fire before winking out as he fell forward, collapsing in a limp heap. Gabriel took a step toward him when a strong wind swept over the plateau, knocking him and Lucifer to the ground. The force dragged them across the dusty land, tumbling them like weeds toward the altar. Michael reached for Gabriel's hand, snagging his wrist as he slid past.

Gabriel grabbed Lucifer, keeping him from flying onto the platform, as the air swirled around Abaddon, finally breaking through the man's barrier. Abaddon screamed, blasting at the clouds, coloring them a bloody red. More thunder bellowed from above, a funnel appearing around the fallen angel. He disappeared amidst the gray, the swirling mass lifting off the altar then across the caked earth. It spun toward Kei, hovering over a small object resting beside the mage before being sucked down, nothing but a flash of red light making its demise.

Gabriel released Lucifer as the winds dissipated, dust and debris settling around them. Gabriel stumbled to his feet, sprinting across the distance before falling to his knees. Greyson's book fluttered from the gust of air, the pages rustling then stilling. Gabriel lifted Kei into his lap, brushing the man's hair from his face as he thumbed his cheek. Kei's pale skin glared up at him, the lack of color like a knife to Gabriel's soul.

He probed their connection, breath held tight as he waited for the echo of his mate's heartbeat. "Kei?"

CHAPTER NINETEEN

"Kei!"

Kei rolled his head to the side, wincing as pain ricocheted through his skull, beating like a drum inside his head. Strong fingers caressed his cheeks, the sensuous touch coaxing him to open his eyes. He blinked away the fuzziness, staring into Gabe's blue gaze.

The man smiled, dipping down and taking Kei's mouth with his. Gabe didn't seize control, choosing to linger with their lips pressed together, tongues gently exploring. A throat cleared off to their right, the sound easing Gabe back.

Kei shifted his focus, groaning when the simple movement spun the landscape. He grabbed onto Gabe's arm in an effort to ground himself, cursing when his vision did another revolution.

"Oh bloody hell."

Kei managed to focus just as Lucifer knelt beside him, cupping his head as he released a sharp blast of energy into him. It jerked him upright, shattering the dizzy feeling as the other man's power prickled Kei's skin. The scenery stabilized, the pounding in his head fading.

Gabriel glared at Lucifer. "Have you heard of gentle?"

Lucifer shrugged. "Humans refer to me as 'the devil'. I don't do gentle." He stood, crossing his arms over his chest. "So, Kei..." He drew out Kei's name as if it held some special meaning. "Where'd you put our boy?"

Kei relaxed into Gabe when the man shuffled Kei against his chest. "Someplace safe."

Lucifer merely stared at him.

Kei sighed. "Fine. I trapped him in Greyson's spell book. Hell of a trick if I do say so."

Lucifer glanced at the tome lying open on the ground before nudging it with his foot. "You trapped him with a spell? Inside a book?"

Kei grinned. "You said it had to be somewhere he couldn't access his power. Trust me. He can't do shit unless he's released. And I'm thinking we burn that reversal spell, just to be safe."

Lucifer stared at the fluttering pages, the gleam in his eyes sending a cold shiver down Kei's spine. The man bent over, picking up the tome as he flicked through the pages, stopping at the back. He laughed, shaking his head before looking at Gabriel and Michael. Indecision seemed to cloud the man's eyes before he sighed.

He held the volume out to Michael. "As much as I'd love to keep this on my shelf... Some of my associates have been known to be...untrustworthy. Thinking you might know of a safe place."

Michael took the book, staring at Lucifer as if he'd never seen the man before.

Lucifer gawked at him. "What?"

Michael shrugged. "It's just...unlike you."

"If Abaddon gets loose again, he'll destroy Hell along with everything else. And I've grown quite fond of the place." He took a step back. "I'll reiterate. I don't like it when someone tries to take what's mine." His gaze swung to Michael. "Don't take this the wrong way, big brother, but...you're looking a bit worse for wear. And it doesn't really stroke my ego to kick your ass when it's not a fair fight. We can go a few rounds next time." Lucifer snapped his fingers, vanishing in a whoosh of air.

Michael mumbled under his breath, turning to face them. His gaze centered on Gabriel as he knelt to their level. "Lucifer was right about one thing. That was quite the risk you took—summoning him. Then locking Abaddon inside a book. There were a thousand ways it could have gone wrong."

Kei grinned, nodding at Gabe. "Only needed one of them to go right."

Michael chuckled. "I see why Gabriel chose you." He tilted his head to the side. "About your grace..."

Gabe waved his concern away. "Still there, just... different." He winked at Kei. "Better."

Michael nodded, tapping the book as he straightened. "I should go put this somewhere safe. Then I'll come back and help clean up." His focus swung to Orifiel. "Though I don't relish the fallout from this."

Gabe looked at his brother, unconscious on the ground. "I think there's been enough falling, don't you?" He smiled at Michael. "Someone once told me...it's in our nature to forgive."

"I'll remember that." He took a few steps back,

spreading his wings as he motioned toward Kei. "I can't wait until you introduce him to Father."

The man launched into the sky, quickly disappearing into the dark.

Kei's mouth gaped open as he stared at where Michael had been standing, replaying the man's parting words. He turned to Gabe, knocking him in the chest with his elbow. "Introduce me to your...Father?"

Gabe chuckled. "Breathe, Kei."

"You try breathing..." He shook his head. "Michael. Lucifer. Your family is...unique."

"Because of you, I met the King of the Faeries. Speaking of which..."

Gabe eased out from behind Kei, crawling over to Greyson. He placed his hands on the man's temples, slowly exhaling as his skin began to glow.

"Whoa, easy there, buddy." Kei grabbed his wrists, gently pulling him back. "Wouldn't do Greyson much good to have you launch him across the plateau."

Gabe huffed. "I'll never gain control if I don't practice. The man's unconscious."

"And the aim is to heal him. Not kill him so you now have to raise him from the dead. Which, theoretically, I'm pretty sure you can do." He smiled at Gabe. "Besides, there's more than a few ways I'd love to have you practice on me."

Gabe's gaze dropped to Kei's groin, a smug grin curving his lips.

Kei placed one palm on Greyson's chest, reaching for Gabriel with the other. "Hold my hand." He chuckled at Gabe's arched brow. "Your power is more playful when it's touching mine. This way, I can draw some without weakening you or jerking Greyson off the ground."

Gabe threaded his fingers through Kei's, the warm feel of his skin calming Kei. He muttered a spell, channeling his energy into the fae. Greyson gasped, his back arching off the dirt before curling back down, a muted groan teasing his lips.

He rolled his head, blinking open his eyes before giving Kei a weak smile. "I'm a genius, aren't I? It worked. They both worked."

Kei shook his head. "I'm thinking we're both just lucky."

"Lucky's just another word for skill." He groaned again as he tried to sit up. He nodded at Gabe. "Those swords you have pack quite the punch."

Gabe shrugged. "I suggest you stay on the other side of them in the future."

"Thanks for the tip, angel..." His voice trailed off as the air snapped around them, Michael appearing in a flash of golden light.

He glanced at Greyson, tilting his head before turning to Gabriel. "I've secured the book. God-willing, no one shall ever find it." He motioned to Greyson, an odd expression shaping his features—as if he'd never seen a faery before. "Are you well, Greyson of the Fae?"

Greyson held up his hands. "Kei already healed me. I'm fine."

"Very well." Michael reached for his sword, offering it to Gabriel. "Your sword, brother. It served me well."

Gabe clapped Michael on the back. "It would honor me if you'd keep it. Greyson has a sword I can use, if the need arises."

Michael closed his eyes, seemingly gathering his composure before nodding. "I'll see you get another. But until then..." He walked over to Orifiel, lifting the man and draping him over his shoulder. "I don't suppose you know where I can find Uriel?"

Kei sighed. "He's at my place. Trapped in a blood fire circle."

Amusement tilted Michael's lips. "Then perhaps we should allow him more time to...contemplate his redemption. Gabriel. Kei..." He paused then nodded. "Greyson." He took off again, the air snapping in his wake.

Greyson whistled. "Got to hand it to you, Kei. You have the best adventures."

Kei grunted. "I'll be happy just to sleep without worrying about demons stabbing me in the back for a while."

"Which reminds me..." Greyson pushed to his feet, swaying slightly before gaining his balance. "Seeing as you're sort of in limbo for a bit, what with Gabriel needing to learn some control..."

Kei inhaled as the pressure increased around them. "Greyson. I don't think you're strong enough to..."

The scenery shifted, a small room blurring into view amidst Greyson's blue light. Kei caught his balance on Gabe's arm, his stomach tumbling into his boots.

He glared at Greyson. "Damn it, Grey. You really need to stop doing that. I mean it."

Greyson waved Kei's concern away. "Give it a century. You'll get used to it." He motioned to the space. "So, what do you think?"

Kei looked around. A large bed dominated the area, the

ornate carvings along the posts catching his attention. He walked over to it, smoothing his hands along the wood. "This is amazing. Where are we?"

"Your bedroom. Well...yours and Gabriel's. The rest of the home is through there." He pointed to a door. "It's next to mine, in case you were wondering."

"Our place?" Kei furrowed his brow. "But why—"

"You two pretty much prevented one version of the apocalypse. To put it mildly, my dad's grateful. He thought you might want to call this place home... Whenever you're visiting, that is. Which he hopes you'll do often." Greyson beamed. "If you ask me, he's quite taken with Gabriel. Thinks it's interesting having an archangel as a friend."

"That's...most generous, but Oberon doesn't have to—"

"My father doesn't do anything that isn't in his heart. Believe me. I know. So is that a yes?"

Gabriel stepped forward, bowing his head slightly. "Tell your king we'd be most honored to accept his gift."

"Sweet!" Greyson spun then paused, glancing back at them. "Oh, and you might want to...you know...seal the home. Or at least this room. Faeries have a penchant for... watching. And you two are definitely worth pulling up a chair for."

"Greyson!" Kei moved toward the man only to have him laugh as he winked out, a shimmering blue hue lingering in the air. "I swear, one day, I'm going to strangle that bastard."

Gabriel snugged up behind him, wrapping his arms around Kei's chest. "He's...unique."

"He's an ass."

"I'm starting to think that's a good thing." Gabe nuzzled Kei's ear. "Or maybe it's just your ass that's a good thing."

Gabe's skin glowed as he muttered some words, waving his hand around the room. "There. That should keep your fae friends out. At least, for a while. Though knowing how skilled they are in the ancient texts—we might want to learn some new warding techniques. Unless it excites you knowing they might be watching us."

Kei's breath hitched as Gabe smoothed his hands down Kei's torso, tracing every dip and angle until he reached his waist. He thumbed the button on Kei's pants, popping it free before lowering the zipper. His hand dipped beneath the fabric, his fingers wrapping around Kei's erection.

Gabe hummed in Kei's ear. "I think this is the first time you've allowed me to undress you. I'm discovering I rather like it."

Kei let his head fall against Gabe's shoulder as the man pumped his shaft, using his other hand to shove Kei's pants over his hips. The material hit the floor, puddling at Kei's feet as Gabriel held him close, slowly working his cock as if they had nothing but time.

"We have all the time we need." Gabe nipped at his neck, muttering under his breath.

Kei chuckled as his shirt vanished along with the other garments. "I thought you liked undressing me?"

"Took too long. I like having your skin on mine more." He skimmed one hand up Kei's torso, plucking at Kei's nipple with his fingers.

"God, Gabe."

"Not quite, but I'll let that one slide."

"Jackass."

"There's that word again. Ass. I can assure you, I have big plans for yours. But first…"

Gabriel's skin started to glow again, the air thickening around them. Kei glanced at his mate a moment before his body lifted off the ground, his limbs held firm to either side. He glanced around, frowning when Gabe moved in front of him, one hand cupping his elbow as he tapped a finger against his lips.

The man nodded. "Yes. I quite like that. Not too high, but nicely spread out for me." He moved in close, his head even with Kei's. "How did you phrase it…I think I'm getting a handle on this sharing thing?"

Kei arched his brow. "Not bad for a first time. Now, let me down and we can get started."

"Oh, trust me. We've already started. And I have no intentions of letting you down until you've screamed my name so loud, your fae friends will hear despite the wards I placed around the room."

"You're going to fuck me while I'm…stuck like this."

"Suspended. Two entirely different things. You have Greyson to thank for this. He gave me the idea when he said he'd expected to find one of us pinned to something."

"But I'm not pinned. I'm floating."

"Even better." He disappeared behind Kei. "Gives me complete access."

"Gabriel…" His voice rasped into a groan as Gabe's wings teased his back, caressing their way down to his feet then up again. The feathers swirled across his skin, leaving a wake of goosebumps.

Kei breathed out, trying to crush his moan of approval

and failing. "Damn, Gabe. If your idea of foreplay is touching me with your wings..." He let his head bow toward his chest as the man drew one wing tip between his legs. "Christ. So damn good."

"I thought you'd eventually see it my way." He moved in front again, pressing his body tight to Kei's as he brushed his lips over Kei's mouth. "Thank you."

Kei forced his brain to process the words. "Thank you? For what?"

"For saving my grace. Then saving me from it."

"My pleasure. At least, I hope it's going to be, because if you strand me here without holding true to your promise..."

"I'm an archangel. I'm bound to my word." He mouthed Kei's neck, sending a shiver down his spine. "As surly as I'm bound to you."

"Good, because I plan on reciprocating the favor as soon as you let me down." He looked Gabriel in the eye. "Love you."

"Love you more. Now be a good mage, and set me on fire."

EXCERPT ~ MICHAEL

What am I doing?

Michael groaned inwardly as he stood at the edge of the pond, staring at the shore across from him. Sunlight danced along the calm surface, reflecting the sinking orb on the distant horizon. Frogs called to each other in the tangle of reeds at the edge of the water, the low sound adding to the surreal atmosphere of the glen. A light breeze rustled the feathers on his wings, tousling his hair across his face, and for a moment, his reasons for visiting the faery realm didn't seem so crazy.

A door creaked open behind him, followed by the pad of footsteps across the stone path. The noises around Michael paused, almost as if the surrounding land was taking a long, slow breath before picking up, again, the constant chatter not as peaceful as it had been seconds before. A sigh lit the air, followed by a disgruntled huff.

"Tell me, Michael. How long are you going to stand there, avoiding him?"

Michael sighed under his breath before glancing

over his shoulder. Gabriel leaned against a tree, his silhouette illuminated by the warm light of his brother's cottage. The angel's shadow stretched out in front of him, the edges joining with the darkness on the soft grass. His grace shimmered around him—not quite as luminous as it'd once been. More of a muted fluorescence than the blinding light Michael knew surrounded him. A testament to the combined energy of Gabriel and his mate Kei—a fire mage whose magic had been woven through his brother's grace when the sorcerer had inadvertently saved Gabriel from falling. Though Michael guessed Gabriel hadn't minded the way the event had turned out—Kei and Gabriel. Together.

Michael looked back at the setting sun, watching the different shades of orange and yellow chase each other across the sky. He'd spent more than a few nights watching the sphere dip below the horizon—enjoying the simple pleasures he'd allowed to slip away. Vowing to make the most of his second chance.

Pain and anger churned in his gut. He'd nearly died at the hands of Abaddon. If it hadn't been for Gabriel, Kei and Greyson, Michael never would have survived. A chuckle sounded inside his head. Lucifer. His brother had been the one to free Michael from Abaddon's cage. Had healed him when Gabriel had been unable, and that one act had opened a channel between them. Not that Michael couldn't block the other man. He just didn't seem to have the energy most days. Penance for not being strong enough. For allowing his complacency to cloud his judgment. Blind him from seeing what had been festering around him for years.

He drew a deep breath. "I think Kei's love of fire has melted your brain, brother. You're talking nonsense."

Gabriel snorted. "Still in denial, I see."

Michael huffed as the other angel moved in beside him, the man's gaze taking in the colors staining the clouds. "There's nothing to deny. I was just watching the sun set. Something I've taken for granted for far too long."

"No, you were trying to catch a glimpse of Greyson as he headed out for his nightly patrol."

It was no secret that Greyson checked the various portals dotted along the perimeter each day, a fact that had made watching the fae dangerously easy.

Michael shrugged off the comment. "The portals have been warded, even against us. If Greyson hadn't given me a means of bypassing them, I wouldn't be here. Which means he doesn't need to perform nightly checks."

"We both know Greyson sees it differently. Ever since Uriel popped in for an uninvited visit, he's been obsessively vigilant about security."

Michael nodded, despite the jab of guilt. Just another way he'd failed as God's Warrior. He'd allowed Uriel to destroy parts of the faery realm. Kill some of Greyson's people. And Michael knew it was a burden he'd never truly shed. "That's not his cross to bear."

Gabriel arched a brow. "Nor is it yours."

Michael huffed, staring at the water, again, when the door behind them opened and closed. Another shadowed silhouette moved across the ground. Michael didn't need to turn to know Kei had joined them. His brother's mate was rarely far away, especially with them still learning how to share their power.

Kei gave Michael a pat on his shoulder before stopping

in front of Gabriel. He leaned into the other angel's chest as Gabriel wrapped one arm around his upper torso. "What is it with you angel types and all the guilt?"

Michael glanced at the mage. "I'm merely shouldering what is ultimately mine. If I hadn't allowed Abbadon to imprison me—"

"The guy was crazy. No one's responsible for his decisions, but him. And I doubt either of you would have believed your own brothers would rise against you."

"Regardless..." Michael glanced away. Arguing with Kei and Gabriel was about as effective as arguing with Greyson. Stubborn didn't begin to describe their joint personalities.

He raised his chin. "So, why allow Greyson to continue his obsession?"

Kei laughed. "He's about as reasonable as you are. But you're only lying to yourself if you think he's this vigilant because he's afraid something might get past his wards."

"Then, why make the nightly rounds?"

Kei's lips lifted into an amused smile. "Maybe because he's got ulterior motives for following such a strict, dare I say, predictable schedule."

Michael ignored the insinuation. "I'm sure having an archangel lay waste to your homeland changes your priorities."

"Please. I've known Grey for decades. Trust me. Not much gets to him. Which brings me back to my hypothesis that he's not scouring the borderlands for the good of his people."

"Why else would he spend all that time alone?"

Gabriel rolled his eyes. "Probably because he's hoping he won't be alone for long."

Michael released a weary breath, allowing his head to bow to his chest as his shoulders drooped. "Gabriel…"

"Why are you making this so difficult? I saw the way Greyson looked at you. Not to mention the fact he finds a way to bring you up in damn near every conversation. And while I know the reasons for his people giving Kei and me a home here are pure, he doesn't visit us as often as he does because he lacks for companionship. He's hoping my brother will drop by."

Michael glanced at him. "Did he tell you that?"

Kei groaned, pulling free of Gabriel's embrace to fully face Michael. "He didn't have to. The guy's an open book. But what I find puzzling is why you come here then hide your presence from him."

"It's…complicated."

Gabriel nudged him. "What's so complicated? He likes you, you like him…"

"I'm an archangel."

Gabriel laughed. "As am I."

"You're…different."

"Why?" Gabriel's gaze slid to Kei. "Because I have a mate? Or because I'm not as pure as I used to be?"

"I didn't mean…" Michael raked a hand through his hair as his wings fluttered with impatience. This wasn't going the way he'd hoped, not that talking about Greyson was ever a direction Michael enjoyed going. The fae clouded Michael's judgment. Made him consider paths he'd never imagined he'd choose. Made him dream of a life he couldn't have.

He crossed his arms over his chest, hoping to change the subject. "What you and Kei have…it's a bond very few of us will ever find. It makes you special."

"I'm not special, brother. I just listened to my heart instead of all the reasons I shouldn't let my mate in."

"I'm a warrior."

Kei shrugged. "So's Grey."

Michael threw up his hands, stomping away before spinning. "He's a prince. Heir to the throne. His father is practically a god."

"And yours is." Gabriel gave him a small smile. "The only difference between us, Michael, is that I wasn't afraid to make myself vulnerable. To admit that there's someone else who means more to me than...me."

"Don't you mean your job? Your faith?"

"It doesn't have to be like that. I still serve Father as I did before. I'm just not a slave to that faith. I see the bigger picture, and so can you."

"I'm God's Warrior. I can't put my own happiness, my needs, above those of His children."

"If Father didn't want us to fall in love, we wouldn't have fated mates lurking around, waiting for us to find them."

Michael glanced across the pond as a man appeared on the far side. The fae paused, lifting his head to the sky before letting it fall to his chest as he trudged off. Even this far away, Michael knew it was Greyson. He felt the other man's soul beckoning to him like a beacon. Heard the echoed beat of Grey's heart thrum in his head. Michael's wings twitched, again, and he had to fist his hands at his side to stop from simply taking to the sky—closing the distance between them.

Gabriel cupped his shoulder. "Greyson's a good man. A worthy man."

"He's not a man, and I'm afraid I'm the one who

isn't worthy. If you and Kei hadn't intervened...I'd be dead."

"And if Kei hadn't accidentally summoned me, so would I."

"I don't think it was an accident."

"The point is, we all played a part. You saved us equally, I assure you."

Michael shook his head. "All I did was look like a fool."

"Michael—"

"I had to have Lucifer heal me. He broke the cage's warding. *Lucifer*. And he didn't even ask for anything in return. Do you know how that gnaws at me?"

Gabriel released a weary breath. "Lucifer isn't our enemy. He's our brother. While I realize his past isn't exemplary, he's still family. And if I've learned anything from my time in this realm, it's that family matters. Greyson would never hold that against you. In fact, it was his idea to summon the man, which leads me to think he doesn't have any issues with Lucifer being your brother." Gabriel squared his shoulders, drawing himself up. "As I recall, Lucifer healed Kei, as well. And I'm thankful for it."

"That's different. Kei nearly died summoning Lucifer. He owed your mate."

"Now, you're just grasping at excuses. This has nothing to do with Lucifer or Father and everything to do with the fact you're scared."

"Of course, I'm scared. If Abaddon can get to me, if my own brothers can cast me out—"

"You're an archangel. There's always going to be someone who has a grievance with you."

"Then you know why I can't ask Greyson to give himself to me. Not when I know there are more than a few entities who'd love to use my feelings against me. He'd be a target."

"And you think Kei isn't? Need I remind you that Greyson chose to accompany us. To face Abaddon. He doesn't scare easily." Gabriel motioned to where Greyson had reappeared across the water. "Whether he wants to take the risk is his choice."

"Not if he never knows how I feel." Michael held up his hand, once again, fighting the urge to take to the sky and join the other man on the opposite side of the water. "It's better this way. Without me...he'll be free to find someone who can give him what he needs."

"All he needs is for you to let him in. To love him despite the odds. The risks. It's all any of us can ask for. And often more than we deserve."

"He'll find someone else. Someone far more worthy than I."

Gabriel grabbed his wrist when Michael turned to leave. "Faeries aren't that different from us, Michael. He only has one true soul, as well."

"Then, it's best I leave so he can find it."

"Michael—"

Michael ignored Gabriel's call as he took off, heading for the portal back to his world. To where there was order. Peace. The sharp pain through his chest didn't mean anything, least of all that he cared for the fae.

ABOUT THE AUTHOR

Author, single mother, slave to chaos—she's a jack-of-all-trades who's constantly looking for her ever elusive clone.

And don't forget to subscribe to her newsletter to get the latest scoop on new and upcoming releases as well as exclusive free reads.

https://www.subscribepage.com/krisnorris

Kris loves connecting with fellow book enthusiasts. You can find her on these social media platforms...

krisnorris.ca
contactme@krisnorris.ca

f facebook.com/kris.norris.731
🐦 twitter.com/kris_norris
📷 instagram.com/girlnovelist
a amazon.com/author/krisnorris

www.ingramcontent.com/pod-product-compliance
Lightning Source LLC
Chambersburg PA
CBHW050030180626
46810CB00002B/649